"Come on, you lovely girl, there's no need for tears."

Alex passed her a handkerchief. "I've known some women to cry at the end of a love affair," he continued wryly, "but not before it's even started!"

"I don't want an affair with you!" Lorna blew her nose fiercely and tried to stop her hands from shaking.

"Oh yes, you do."

The calm certainty in his voice brought a rising tide of anger to Lorna's aid. Jumping to her feet, she tossed back her hair and glared at him. "One fine day, Lord Kendall, it's going to dawn on you that you aren't God's gift to women. I hope you manage to survive the shock!"

"Bravo!" Alex exclaimed. "But you really must learn to stop fighting both me and you, Lorna. We'll be a lot happier if you do."

Books by Mary Lyons

These books may be available at your local bookseller.

Don't miss any of our special offers. Write to us at the following address for information on our newest releases.

Harlequin Reader Service
P.O. Box 52040, Phoenix, AZ 85072-2040
Canadian address: P.O. Box 2800, Postal Station A,
5170 Yonge St., Willowdale, Ont. M2N 6J3

MARY LYONS

eclipse of the heart

Harlequin Books

TORONTO • NEW YORK • LONDON
AMSTERDAM • PARIS • SYDNEY • HAMBURG
STOCKHOLM • ATHENS • TOKYO • MILAN

Harlequin Presents first edition October 1985
ISBN 0-373-10828-1

Original hardcover edition published in 1985
by Mills & Boon Limited

CHAPTER ONE

OUTSIDE, in the courtyard of the Louvre Palace, gusts of wind and rain buffeted the canvas walls of the large marquees, while inside one of the huge tents, crammed full to overflowing, the sheer volume of noise was deafening. As the models strode swiftly up and down the raised catwalk the crowd shouted their approval of the clothes being displayed, their applause vying with the music blaring forth from the loud speakers and muffling the screamed instructions from the hard-eyed fashion editors who were trying to direct their photographers clustered around the platform. Suddenly the lights dimmed, leaving only a blue spotlight to illuminate a tall, slim figure modelling Leo Mondrain's final design: the bridal gown which traditionally concluded most of the Paris Ready to Wear collections.

Gliding slowly down the catwalk to the strains of the wedding march from Lohengrin, Lorna tried to keep her eyes from blinking at the flash of the photographer's bulbs, staring out beyond the serried ranks to some imaginary spot on the far wall of the marquee. The heat and noise were so mind-shattering, it was proving difficult to concentrate on her role: that of interpreting Mondrain's creation so successfully, that for a few minutes the sophisticated audience would indeed believe that they were watching a shy, hesitant bride on her way to her wedding.

Swathed from head to toe in a long hooded cloak of white ermine and holding a small nosegay demurely in front of her; it was only when she reached the end of the platform, throwing the flowers into the audience and allowing the sumptuous fur cloak to slip from her

5

bare shoulders, that the onlookers could see the creation she was modelling.

Incredulous gasps and cries of excitement greeted Lorna's slowly revolving figure as she displayed the skin-tight, white satin dress, heavily embroidered with pearls and diamonds, and whose minimal strapless bodice barely covered her breasts.

'Really, Leo!' Lorna had protested before the show. 'It will only need one deep breath for me to burst out of that dress. What's more, the skirt is unbelievably tight, I'll never be able to walk up and down the catwalk without falling flat on my face!'

'*Mais, non,* my darling. You will look wonderful, as always!' Leo had purred in reply. 'And if you should "burst out" as you put it—just think what a sensation it will make!'

'Great! Thanks!' Lorna grumbled, but only half-heartedly. Not only had Leo been the first of the great Parisian designers for whom she had worked, but she loved his clothes and they both knew that she would give of her best during the show that morning.

Now, as the music changed to a faster, up-beat tempo, she began to retrace her steps back up the platform. Hardly daring to take a breath, and swaying sensually as she portrayed a modern, liberated version of the traditional bride, the audience erupted as Lorna carelessly dragged the priceless fur cloak on the floor behind her. Frantic screams of *'Bravo!'* and *'Mondrain!'* assaulted her ears as she reached the end of the catwalk, turning with a smile to take Leo's hand and lead him forward to accept his well-deserved ovation.

'It's a great success, Leo. Congratulations!' she whispered, leaning over to kiss his cheek.

'You see, my darling. I told you all would be well with that dress, hmm? *Mon dieu!* She is one terrible old witch!' he muttered from the side of his mouth as he bestowed a wide, beaming smile on the hatchet-faced editor of one of America's foremost fashion magazines.

Entering the turbulent chaos of the backstage changing room, Lorna was pounced upon by a dresser who quickly helped to strip off the bridal gown. Naked, save for a pair of brief panties, she gave a deep sigh of relief at being released from the constricting dress, before forcing her way through the crowd to a corner where her own clothes were hanging on a rail. Climbing into a loose-fitting khaki jump-suit, she went over to sit down in front of the brilliantly lit dressing table which ran the length of the tent.

Slowly removing her make-up, she could feel the tension and excitement draining from her body, leaving her feeling tired and weary. It was always like this after a show, she reminded herself. It was exactly the same reaction she had experienced backstage after a performance in the theatre. Leaning back in her chair she looked in the mirror which clearly reflected the chaotic scene behind her. It's like a cattle market, or maybe a harem, she thought as one half-nude body after another passed across her vision. In her early days as a professional show model, it had taken her some time to become used to the sight of so much naked flesh. Lorna smiled ruefully, remembering how on her first job she had trembled with embarrassment, sheltering behind a large rack of dresses as she tried to change from one garment into another. She had very quickly learnt that during a collection, speed was of the essence, and that no one was the slightest bit interested in the sight of her nudity. During a show, when there was sometimes less than two minutes in which she would have to remove an intricately draped evening gown, replacing it with a formal ensemble which might consist of a suit, blouse, top coat and hat, there was simply no time for modesty.

'My God! It's just like the black hole of Calcutta in here!'

She turned to smile up at her friend, Candice, whose apartment she shared when working in Paris. The tall Texan girl slid her long legs into a pair of tight-fitting black jeans, pulling on a baggy T-shirt before she came to sit down on a chair beside Lorna.

'Whew—I'm whacked!' Candice gave a tired yawn. 'You know, I really hate these tents, they just don't seem to have any atmosphere somehow. Life was a lot more fun when the *Prêt-à-porter* shows were held all over the city. Now, here we are, all crammed into this place—it's a real drag!'

Lorna shrugged. 'Mondrain was telling me that holding the shows here in the Louvre Palace, is all to do with the French Governemnt wanting to promote the prestige of French fashion. They've got a big export drive going on at the moment, apparently.'

'Big deal!'

'Well, considering the prices they charge for the clothes, it probably is a big deal!' Lorna grinned. 'And you must admit that it has to be better than all those frantic dashes from one showroom to another. It used to cost me a fortune to hire a cab and keep it waiting all day, just so that I would be sure of arriving at the various shows in plenty of time. For instance,' she added, 'we've got Saint Laurent's collection to do next, and now we only have to walk over to one of the other marquees. It's a breeze!'

'I suppose you're right,' Candice sighed. 'But why on earth do we do it? The job, I mean. I seem to be spending half my life here in Paris, when if I had any sense at all, I'd be back in the States getting ready to have a nice lunch with my boyfriend—not sitting here in this crummy place.' She looked glumly around at the crowded confusion of models, fitters, design assistants and hairdressers, all shouting at the top of their voices as they packed up the clothes and their equipment.

'The money!' Lorna murmured, drawing a brush through her long dark gold hair and staring at her reflection with cool indifference. Others might see beauty in her face, but she was only too well aware of the flaws: the slant of her wide green eyes, which gave her a curiously secretive, cat-like expression; the high cheek bones and long straight nose; and above all, her wide mouth with its full lower lip hinting at passionate sexuality. She had learned over the years how to make the best of her imperfect features, but beyond the facial care and attention needed for her job, she took very little interest in her face, regarding it solely as a helpful, necessary tool for her profession.

'Huh?' Candice queried, feeling a pang of envy as she gazed in the mirror at the girl beside her. Despite the harsh lighting and the fact that Lorna wasn't wearing a trace of make-up, nothing it seemed could dim her striking bone structure and startling good looks.

'The money,' repeated Lorna, bending down to put her things away in a large tote bag. 'We do it for the money—and the clothes, of course. Like the show I did last night for Georges Lassalle, for instance. I knew he hadn't a bean and wouldn't be able to pay me,' she shrugged. 'But, well, I adore his clothes and I felt that I could give them something.'

'Wow! Mercy won't like that,' Candice laughed. 'She really hates it when we work for free!'

Lorna gave a rueful grimace of agreement, recalling her last encounter with their agent. Mercy Bird, of Beautiful Birds Inc., was a tough, thin bean-pole of a woman who owned and ran one of the top agencies in New York, and was quite capable of cutting her models down to size with one of her devasting remarks. 'You've got to cut out these "freebees",' Mercy had warned Lorna in her rasping Bronx voice. 'You aren't getting any younger, kiddo, and it's about time you began to think about your old age pension!'

Mercy was right, of course. Lorna sighed as she realised that her agent had, after all, only been pointing out the unwelcome truth. At twenty-five years of age it was time she started thinking about her future—and Beth's too, of course. She reached inside the pocket of her jump-suit and took out the letter she had received that morning from her sister. Quickly scanning the large scrawl it was clear that nothing dramatic had happened while she had been in Paris. Which made a pleasant change from the last time she had been away, on a modelling trip to Rome. Beth had apparently been so immersed in practising her music, that she had let the bath overflow into the apartment below. The super-intendant of the apartment block had not been amused—and neither had she on receiving the bill for the damage!

'How's that sister of yours?' Candice asked, leaning over her shoulder.

'Beth's fine. She's due to graduate from the Juillard School this summer.'

'Then what's she going to do? Is she still hoping to become a concert pianist?'

'I honestly don't know.' Lorna's forehead creased in a worried frown. Beth had been extraordinarily secretive of late, refusing to discuss her future career and stonewalling any of Lorna's attempts to find out what her sister wanted to do with her life. She had, moreover, become surprisingly reticent about her private life during the last three months, looking pale and drawn. She didn't want to invade Beth's privacy, but clearly something wasn't right . . .

'Oh my God! Look at the time!' Candice jumped hurriedly to her feet. 'We'd better scram. I'll just bet the Directrice at Saint Laurent is doing her nut right now, wondering where we are!'

'There's no need to panic,' Lorna said, calmly zipping up her bag. 'The show is bound to start at least half an hour late, and from all the noise out there, it sounds as if the audience still hasn't even been admitted to the marquee.'

Candice put her head on one side, listening to the muffled shouts of exasperation and abuse. Those lucky enough to possess one of the coveted invitations to view Yves Saint Laurent's collection were pressing themselves against the crash barriers guarding the entrance, and vociferously demanding their immediate admittance.

'Yup—you're right. It sounds just like feeding time at the zoo, doesn't it?' Candice laughed. 'Ah well, *c'est la vie*, I suppose! Come on, Lorna, let's get the next show on the road!'

The weather still hadn't improved when Lorna flew back to New York a week later. Her cab driver complained bitterly all the way from Kennedy airport: 'I've heard of April showers, but I tell ya, this has gotta be ridiculous!' He swerved to avoid a heavy truck, leaning out to inform the truck driver that not only was he a menace on the streets, but that his family background left much to be desired—or impolite words to that effect—which provoked an equally abusive reply from the other driver.

Lorna leaned back in her seat and smiled to herself. Yes, she was back in the Big Apple all right! Glancing out of the window, she saw that there were only a few more blocks to go before the cab reached her apartment overlooking Central Park. It cost her a fortune to live there, but she never regretted her decision of three years ago, and especially not at a time like this when she was feeling so tired and exhausted. In a few minutes she would be able to wind down and relax amidst the familiar and comfortable surroundings. The last weeks had been a strain, and she felt a keen longing to close her own front door and to be alone at last, without fear of interruption or disturbance.

Joe, the head porter, helped to carry her bags across the marble foyer and into the elevator of the apartment building. Opening her front door, she went through into the living room and over to look out of the large window at the stark outlines of the Manhattan sky-scrapers, etched black against the storm clouds which were still visible in the falling dusk of late afternoon.

'Anything else I can do for you, Miss Grant?'

'No, I'm fine. You really shouldn't have insisted on bringing up my cases, Joe.' Lorna pulled the drapes across the window and turned to smile at the elderly man.

'It's my pleasure.' Joe beamed at the tall, almost too slim girl who was running a tired hand through her long gold hair, the colour of very old, very fine cognac. 'Had a long trip?' he asked. 'Where did you go this time—Paris, France?'

Lorna nodded. She was feeling far too weary to try and explain that her itinerary had also included Munich, London and Rome. Opening her purse, she walked over to press some money into his hand.

'Hey, now, there's no need . . .' he protested, looking up into the girl's wide green eyes, curiously flecked with gold. So like her father's, he thought suddenly. Lawrence Grant, the well-known impresario, had taken over the apartment in what was then a new building, the same month Joe had started work there. Those had been the days: the famous people, the parties, and the women—especially the women! Joe sighed with regret for past glories which had ended as suddenly and dramatically as the car smash which had terminated Lawrence Grant's life, some three years ago.

'Nonsense,' said Lorna firmly, shrugging off her coat and tossing it over the back of a chair. 'I could never have hauled everything up here by myself. So, have a drink on me, and don't spend it playing poker or Mabel will go up the wall!'

They both grinned at each other, remembering the times Lawrence, who had suffered from insomnia, had dragged Joe into the apartment during the early hours of the morning to join in a poker game; which had, as often as not, included some of the security guards and anyone else her father could find awake at that time of night. A pastime of which Joe's wife, Mabel, had thoroughly disapproved.

'Mabel's far too wrapped up in our new grandson to worry about something like that!' Joe winked as he turned to leave. 'But, hell, I sure do miss your dad,' he added. 'Things just aren't the same, somehow.'

Half an hour later Lorna finished hanging up her clothes in her bedroom, wandering through into the living room in stockinged feet. Fixing herself a stiff drink, she went over to slump down into a chair and allowed the calm silence of the apartment to seep into her tired mind. Things certainly weren't the same, she thought ruefully, recalling Joe's words. It wasn't just the shock of her father's death which had been so traumatic, but the necessary change in her lifestyle had been equally dramatic. That first meeting with Lawrence's attorneys after the funeral had made matters very clear. Her sister Beth was still away at boarding school in Switzerland, and so Lorna had been alone in the lawyer's office as he had spelled out the hard facts of life; that Lawrence's lifestyle had been lived far and away beyond his earnings, and that he had been existing on credit for the past five years. Everything he had owned was heavily mortgaged or had been put up as collateral for loans which would now have to be repaid. There was no stock, no investments and no capital. In brief, after everything had been sold to meet his debts, including the large holiday home in Maine, there would be no money left.

Suddenly, from having been the pampered, wealthy children of the celebrated and charming Lawrence

Grant, Lorna and Beth now found themselves penniless and their inheritance from their father amounting to nothing more or less than a mountain of debt.

'It doesn't matter about myself, but what about my sister's education?' Lorna had queried in dazed confusion. 'She's got another term at school, and then my father had intended to send her to the Paris Conservatoire. She's—Beth's an excellent pianist,' she had added lamely.

The attorney merely shrugged. 'Your father left no provision for that, I'm afraid. I understand that the apartment, here in New York, forms no part of your father's estate, since he put it in your name some years ago. You could sell it to pay your sister's school fees, of course.'

'But then she'd have no home!' Lorna protested.

The attorney could only shrug his shoulders again and express his regrets that her father had not been more prudent with his financial affairs.

She had left his office in a daze, taking a cab to Central Park and spending the rest of the day walking up and down as she tried to think what to do for the best. Their mother had died when Beth was ten, and since she had been a shy, introverted little girl Lorna, then aged fourteen and a far more outgoing character, had taken her sister under her wing, always being fiercely protective of the younger girl. Besides, her father had always said that Beth was a talented musician, and it therefore was vitally important that she should be allowed to continue with her studies.

Sinking down on to an empty bench, Lorna found herself bitterly regretting that she herself was so ill-equipped to earn her living. Although she had been incredibly lucky to be offered a part in a Broadway theatre production straight from drama school, the years she had spent travelling the motor racing circuits of the world with Carlo meant that she was completely out of touch with her old profession. Who would be likely to give her an acting job now? And even if she was fortunate enough to find a walk-on part somewhere, the pay would be hardly sufficient to support herself and pay Beth's school fees as well. She had to find a answer—she must! Sitting there on the bench that day, Lorna had vowed to herself that she would somehow manage to keep on the apartment and provide for herself and Beth. Amazingly, against all the odds, she had succeeded far better than she could ever have imagined.

With a sigh, Lorna put down her glass, forcing her weary body from the comfortable chair and going through to run herself a bath.

Stripping off her clothes and pinning her hair up on top of her head, she eased herself into the perfumed suds with a deep groan of contentment. There was nothing—absolutely nothing—so wonderful as a long soak in a warm bath, especially after a tiring journey. Modern day air-travel really was the end, she mused, lying back and relishing the sensual softness of the oily water against her skin. The time spent in the air was as nothing to the hassle on the ground; check-in times at airports seemed to be getting longer and longer. While as for the length of time required to claim one's bags at the end of the flight . . .! Thank God for the Air France commercial. She hadn't particularly wanted to do the ad, but when she had been told the fee consisted of six flights a year on the Paris–New York Concorde run, she had leapt at the job. Travelling as much as she did, Lorna deeply appreciated being able to cross the Atlantic in under four hours, and the comfort and service almost made air-travel a pleasure and not the pain it usually was.

She climbed out of the bath, wrapping herself in a warm towel before going over to inspect herself critically in the mirror. The last weeks had been more than hectic, and the strain was clearly evident in the dark circles that she was sure she could see beneath her green eyes. Your face is supposed to be your fortune, but nobody's going to pay a blind cent for the way you look right now! she told herself with a grimace. Slipping into a pale green towelling robe, she put on a face pack, carefully smoothing the white paste over her skin until only her eyes could be seen. She was definitely not, 'a thing of beauty and joy forever,' she thought, trying not to grin as she felt the mask tighten and harden on her cheeks. It would be ten minutes before she could wash it off, and the time might as well be spent usefully. Going back into the living room, she switched on the telephone answering machine. Her agent, Mercy Bird, took all her business calls when she was away, and the taped message she had left, saying that she wouldn't be back until today, should mean that there weren't too many calls to return.

'*Hi, Lorna,*' Mercy Bird's harsh, incisive tones flowed economically and swiftly from the tape. '*No problems workwise, you'll be pleased to hear. You're booked for the Calvin Klein show again, and Ashley Cooper wants you for a two-day photo session next week. Give me a ring tomorrow, OK?*'

Lorna lay back in the chair and closed her eyes. Here we go again—back on the tread-mill once more. Still, she could hardly complain about the fantastic money she was earning, not with so many people out of work nowadays. She pressed the switch again.

'*Jay Holden, here. I hope you got my flowers. I've booked a table at La Caravelle for Wednesday night, and then we'll go on to the "21". I'll pick you up at seven o'clock. 'Bye.*'

Oh Lord—what on earth was she going to do about Jay Holden? She'd only met the famous financier a month ago, but already he seemed to have invaded her busy life. Before she had flown to Paris, he had manoeuvred her into going out to dinner with him practically every night, taking no notice of her plea that her career depended on early nights and a minimal of social life. The whole business was crazy. For one thing, she wasn't sure she even liked the man who seemed to have a finger in practically all the major industries, including airways, tankers, steel and uranium. She certainly wasn't attracted to him physically, and when in his last phone call to Paris he had mentioned taking her to meet his old mother, who lived in a large brownstone mansion on the other side of the Park, alarm bells had rung loudly in Lorna's brain.

Jay was quite interesting to talk to, of course, but that was all as far as she was concerned. The thought of his millions left her cold, and she had told him so one evening, when she had been exasperated beyond measure by his calm assumption that she would drop everything to go out with him. Lorna sighed with frustration as she realised that her sharp rejection of his vast wealth had, if anything, made him even keener on her company. She really must take a firm stand against his steamrollering tactics. Her distracted thoughts were sharply interrupted by a loud ring on the doorbell.

Had Beth forgotten her key again? No, it couldn't be her sister, who she remembered had a late class tonight. And Joe always phoned through before allowing casual visitors to come up. So who . . .? Of course—it must be Jay's flowers, she realised, looking at the empty vases in the living room. She liked to live surrounded by bowls of fresh flowers, but Beth simply wasn't interested and rarely made the effort when Lorna was away.

'Thank you, I . . .' her voice faltered as she pulled open the door to find herself confronted by a tall stranger who quite obviously wasn't carrying a bouquet of flowers. She trembled in panic. Oh, my God! She'd been living in Europe for the past month, and that must be why she had been so incredibly foolish as to open the

door to an unknown man. 'I—um . . .' she muttered
incoherently, inwardly cursing her stupidity in not
having even fixed the door chain when Joe had left the
apartment.

'Miss Grant?' the man asked in a dark, husky drawl.

'Yes.' Lorna relaxed slightly. At least the stranger
seemed to know her name and wasn't a casual mugger
on the prowl. 'Can I help you?'

For the first time since she had opened the door, she
raised her head to take a good look at the man standing
on the threshold. She met a pair of vivid blue eyes set in
a tanned face beneath thick black brows, which were
raised in winged astonishment as he gazed down at the
girl in front of him. He seemed—yes, he definitely
seemed familiar. Where had she seen him before?
Certain that she hadn't met him lately, she frowned as
she tried to search her memory, her action causing the
stiff texture of the mask to pull and crack on her
forehead. Oh no! *She had forgotten the face pack!*
Beneath the white paste her skin burned with
embarrassment, and it was of little comfort to know
that the man couldn't see her blushes.

'I'm sorry, I . . .' she floundered miserably as his eyes
gleamed with cynical amusement.

'It would seem that I have called at an—er—
inauspicious moment,' he murmured. 'However, I
would be grateful for a few minutes of your time.'

Well, if he was a mugger, at least he was a polite one!
And English, too, Lorna realised, her ears registering
the cool, drawling tones of his British accent.

'I'm afraid that I had completely forgotten . . .' she
gestured helplessly at her face, and then was annoyed
with herself for bothering to apologise. Especially since
the strange man was allowing his eyes to conduct an
analytical appraisal, that began at the top of her head
and travelled insolently down her slim figure, to the pink
toe nails of her bare feet. The damned nerve of the man!

Lorna pulled the sides of her robe tightly together to try and hide the deep creamy cleft between her breasts from his sardonic gaze.

'I didn't catch your name,' she said sharply. He was managing to make her feel as if she was standing there naked, and she didn't like it one little bit.

'Possibly because I didn't give it,' he answered, the gleam from his eyes growing more pronounced. 'My name is Kendall.'

'Oh, yes?'

The dark eyebrows lifted again. 'Alex Kendall,' he explained in a bored voice, clearly expecting to be recognised.

Lorna stood looking up at him, the mask hiding all expression on her face. Yes, of course, she should have known who he was. Their paths had never crossed before, but they might easily have done so, since he was involved in her own profession. The extraordinary sense of *déjà vu* she had felt was now crystal clear. She must have seen his face hundreds of times in the gossip columns of the newspapers, both here in New York and abroad. But what, in heaven's name, was the famous photographer, Alex Kendall, doing here? Lord Kendall, to be precise, she reminded herself. A well-known member of the British aristocracy, he was famous for his brilliant photographic portraits and also notorious for his many, well-publicised affairs with beautiful women.

'Oh, yes?' she said blankly again, deciding on the spur of the moment to pretend that she had never heard of him. That would teach him not to go around mentally undressing strange women!

'Won't you let me come in?' he asked, clearly disconcerted by the tone of complete uninterest in her voice.

'I don't see why I should,' Lorna retorted. She was getting cold standing here with the door open and certainly not feeling in the mood to be polite.

'My dear girl, I am hardly likely to steal the family silver!' he mocked, one eyebrow slanted in cynical amusement. 'Besides which, I am quite sure that Harry will have mentioned my name!'

The short, dry bark of sardonic laughter which accompanied his last words baffled Lorna. Harry? The only Harry she knew was Harry Cohen, a literary agent and one of her father's old friends. Why should Harry, whom she hadn't seen for over a year, send this man to see her? Suddenly tired of standing in a draught, Lorna shrugged helplessly, stepping back and allowing him to enter the hall before leading the way back into the living room.

He strolled casually over to the fireplace, looking about him with curiosity. 'This is a very pleasant room—quite charming in fact,' he murmured, not bothering to disguise his surprise as he glanced around at the deep-piled cream carpet and matching raw silk drapes over the large window. The rose-coloured lampshades threw a soft glow over the sofas and chairs covered in pale ice-cream shades of blue, pink and green, the only other form of illumination being that from the lights over the gold frames of the oil paintings on the walls. She saw him glance almost incredulously at a Victorian scene by Millais, before giving an infinitesimal shake of his head and turning to regard the girl standing across the room.

Damned snob! she thought angrily as she accurately read his mind. What had he expected to find in her apartment—bare floor boards? She was just about to tell him that yes, the painting was genuine, as were all the other pictures on the walls, when she thought better of it. After all, he was apparently a friend of Harry Cohen who had always been so kind to her and Beth, and how she invested and spent her money was her own business.

'If you don't mind waiting for a moment, I'll just go and wash this guck off,' she told him, escaping back into the bathroom and sponging the paste from her face.

Don't forget that Pride is one of the seven deadly sins, she lectured herself firmly as she unpinned and brushed out her long gold hair. She was accustomed to being looked at with admiration, and although she hoped she wasn't vain, the sardonic, cynical amusement in Alex Kendall's eyes had definitely raised her hackles. There wasn't much she could do about her robe, but there was no way she was going back to face that arrogant man—not without putting on some mascara and lipstick, she wasn't!

Returning to the living room, she found Alex Kendall seated at his ease in one of the deep arm chairs. Despite being clothed in the most expensive tailoring, nothing could hide his air of leashed, forceful vitality as he stretched his long legs casually out in front of him. None of his photographs in the newspapers had reproduced the restless, physical aura he projected. His vivid blue eyes narrowed as he subjected her changed appearance to an intense scrutiny, the atmosphere in the room seeming to become suddenly charged with electricity.

Lorna found his gaze disturbing, and decided that it would take very little for her to find herself actively disliking the man lounging so casually across the room. As for his amorous reputation, she totally failed to see how any woman would find him particularly attractive—certainly she didn't.

Allowing none of her thoughts to appear on her face, she returned his stare with a bland, non-committal expression. 'Would you care for a drink?' she asked coolly.

'Scotch and soda, please,' he said, frowning as she walked past him towards a bar in the corner of the room. 'You don't look at all how I had imagined you would. Haven't—haven't we met somewhere before?'

Since her face was regularly on the covers of magazines, he was clearly suffering from the same confusion as she had earlier. 'No, we haven't met,' she answered firmly, placing a glass on the table beside him, before going over to sit in a chair across the room. 'And now,' she added, sipping her own drink, 'perhaps you will tell me why you are here?'

'I may as well be blunt,' he said. 'I certainly didn't want to have to see you. It was only after many urgent requests from Aunt Sophie, and constant nagging by my mother, that I'm here at all. I'm sorry to have to tell you that the family are not at all happy about your relationship with Harry.'

'Aren't they?'

'No—and I must admit that I am also totally opposed to the idea of you and Harry getting married.'

'Oh dear—that's a pity!' Lorna murmured, trying with difficulty to keep her face straight. The very idea of her marrying Harry Cohen was screamingly funny! Not only was he almost sixty, but he was happily married with children and grandchildren.

'You seem to be taking it all very coolly,' he commented with a frown.

'Why not?' Lorna shrugged, sipping her drink. This man, Alex Kendall, was quite clearly off his rocker, and while the situation might be amusing, she was nevertheless becoming increasingly annoyed by his contemptuous tone of voice. 'Leaving aside Harry—and not forgetting *dear* Aunt Sophie too, of course—maybe you had better tell me just what business it is of yours who I decide to marry?'

'I'm very fond of Harry and I don't want to see him hurt.' Alex's voice became hard and determined, the strong lines of his tanned face tightening in anger as he brushed his hand through his dark hair. 'Before I came here, I had completely misunderstood the position. I had no idea of the sort of woman I would have to be dealing with!'

'Really?' she enquired sweetly, gritting her teeth and trying to suppress her rising fury.

'Yes, really!' he growled. 'What on earth does a woman like you want with a mere boy? Harry's only twenty-two, while you—you're obviously an experienced and sophisticated woman of the world. You may well be desperate to get married, but why don't you pick on someone of your own age?'

I could hit him! One more word from this contemptuous, arrogant man, and I will definitely not be responsible for my actions! Lorna promised herself. She couldn't remember when she had last felt so angry. How dare he oil his way into her apartment, and then sit lounging in one of her chairs handing out such insults?

'I think that it is about time you crawled back into whatever nasty little hole you emerged from!' she snapped, rising to her feet and walking across the room towards the hall.

Jumping to his feet, he strode swiftly over the thick carpet, grasping her arm with steely fingers and swinging her around to face him with such force that she found herself pinned up against his hard firm chest.

'You really don't give a damn—do you? What is it you want? The title?' he ground out through clenched teeth, his face dark with rage. 'Let me tell you, my dear Beth Grant, that while Harry may be my heir at the moment, I myself am only thirty-six and may yet get married. What will you do then—divorce him I suppose? Well, I'm not prepared to stand by and see Harry's engagement, to a very nice girl in England, just swept aside by some title-chasing harpy! Why don't you just concentrate on your piano, and leave my cousin alone?'

Lorna gazed up at him in bemused stupefaction. He—*he must think that she was Beth!* She shook her head distractedly, trying to reassess the situation. It was quite clear that at no point in their extraordinary conversation had he been referring to Harry Cohen; and really, if she hadn't been so full of dislike of Alex Kendall, she would have seen that long before now. Her heart sank as she tried to think of what sort of mess Beth could have got herself into, mixing with this quite dreadful man and his family?

'Well?'

'Well—nothing!' she snapped. 'I'm not impressed by these bully-boy tactics, and I suggest that you take your hands off me immediately! What did you come here to try and do, anyway? Were you intending to buy my sister off, or did you hope to rely on your famous charm? Either way, I am sorry to say that you are likely to be disappointed! Now, let go of me at once!'

Still holding her in a vice-like grip, Alex Kendall stood staring rigidly down into her face. '*Your sister?* Just who in the hell are you?' he breathed.

'I told you to get your hands off me!' she gasped, disturbed despite her anger by his close proximity. 'My name is Lorna Grant and Beth is my younger sister.'

'You bitch! You led me on to suppose . . .'

'Nobody had to lead you anywhere,' she panted, suddenly feeling frightened by the cold fury in his blue eyes. 'You—you had the brass nerve to march in here, laying down what my sister can and cannot do, just as though you were God Almighty and we were dirt beneath your feet!' She shook with rage. 'Well let me tell you, *Lord* Alex Kendall—or whatever it is you call yourself—that neither Beth nor myself are anything like those vacuous nincompoops you seem to spend your life romancing. We—*Oh . . .*'

Lorna's gasp of outrage was stifled by the swift descent of his dark head, his mouth closing over hers and heartlessly crushing her lips in a ruthless, punishing kiss. Trying to move her head away proved fruitless, and she became breathless beneath the force of his lips and her own exertion as she beat her fists against his broad shoulders, vainly trying to be free of him.

Suddenly, it was over. She found herself released as he stepped back, cursing softly and running his hands distractedly through his hair. Lorna stood dazed and trembling for a moment, before lifting her eyes to her tormentor who was looking towards the hall. Following his gaze, she saw with dismay that not only was her sister standing in the doorway, staring at her with astonishment, but that Beth was not alone. From the wide grin on the face of the uniformed messenger clutching a large bouquet of flowers, it was obvious that he, too, had been an interested observer of all that had just taken place!

CHAPTER TWO

CLUTCHING the large bouquet of flowers and stonily
ignoring the messenger boy's cheeky wink, Lorna closed
the front door after his departing figure and walked
slowly back along the hall into the large, modern kitchen.
Tearing off the cellophane wrapping, she placed the
long-stemmed red roses into a tall jug of water, and then
went to stand gazing blindly out of the window. How on
earth could she possibly face going back into the living
room, and having to meet that awful man once again? Still
feeling weak with shock from Alex Kendall's determined
assault, she brushed a shaking, trembling hand across her
bruised lips. Did he always go around treating every
woman he met like that? It might go some way towards
explaining his notorious reputation as an experienced
seducer, but if he thought he could behave in such a
despicable fashion towards her—and get away with it—
he was in for one big surprise!

Still, she reminded herself, sweet though the thought
of revenge might be, it would have to wait for another
time. The present situation would have to be dealt with
first of all, and she really couldn't remain hiding here in
the kitchen all day. For one thing, she didn't see why
she should allow that damned man to drive her out of
her own living room, and for another, she ought to be
back in there supporting Beth. God knows what her
sister had got herself into—and who, in heaven's name,
were 'Harry' and 'Aunt Sophie'? However, it was clear
that Alex Kendall wasn't someone who minced his
words, and she certainly wasn't prepared to allow him
to speak to Beth in the sort of language he had used
towards her. No way!

26

Taking a deep breath, Lorna forced herself to return to the living room, her entrance unnoticed by Alex and Beth who were sitting together on one of the sofas. As she stood looking across the room at the man she was rapidly coming to actively dislike, she began to understand for the first time just why he was apparently so successful with women. It was nothing more or less than simple, unadulterated and almost irresistible charm, she thought sourly. He might not be outstandingly handsome, but watching him smile as he chatted quietly to her sister, even from where she stood, she could feel the effect of his warm, sensual appeal. It was also clear that Beth was not impervious to his attraction, smiling happily as she gazed up into his face with flushed cheeks and sparkling eyes. Lorna could only offer up a thankful prayer that from all he had said previously, it was unlikely that he would be interested in capturing her sister's heart. Which was just as well, she told herself grimly, because there was no doubt at all that Alex Kendall was a very dangerous man as far as women were concerned—dynamite, in fact!

Alex raised his head to see Lorna standing in the doorway. As he rose politely to his feet, Beth smiled happily at her sister. 'It's lovely to have you home again, Lorna, and what an extraordinary coincidence to find Alex here in the apartment!'

'Extraordinary!' Lorna echoed.

Beth was too elated to notice the caustic note in her sister's voice. 'I mean, I had no idea that Harry was related to Alex—isn't it fantastic!'

'Isn't it, just!' Lorna murmured dryly. This time she got the message across—an icy-blue glare from beneath Alex's heavy eyelids indicated as much. Beth looked at her sister in confusion.

'Well, I think it's really great to know that the famous photographer, Alex Kendall, is Lord Kendall

and—and Harry's first cousin.' Beth turned to him.
'Lorna's in the business too, only on the other side of
the camera. She's tremendously well-known and
successful,' she added proudly. 'But how silly of me,
you must already know that!'

Alex gazed intently at Lorna and then clicked his
fingers in annoyance. 'I should have recognised you—
especially since your face is on this month's cover of
Vogue.' He shrugged. 'It wasn't a bad picture at all, but
the lighting was hopelessly wrong, of course.'

Arrogant know-all! Lorna found herself seething with
fury, which wasn't helped by the fact that she had to
acknowledge the swine was quite right. Richard Long
was a potentially brilliant photographer, but his lighting
often left much to be desired.

'But I don't understand. Surely you two know each
other? I mean . . .' Beth's puzzled voice trailed away as
she looked in bewilderment at the rising tide of colour
on her sister's face. Alex Kendall also seemed to be
similarly disconcerted.

'Yes—er—well, actually,' he murmured, 'it was you I
came here to see, Beth. I was somewhat—er—confused,
I'm afraid, and there's no doubt that I owe your sister an
apology.' He turned to smile ruefully at Lorna.

'You certainly do!' That oh-so charming, loathsome
man needn't try and think that he could soft-soap her,
she thought grimly. However, she was grateful for the
support of the door-frame behind her back, since for
some reason Alex's smile had left her feeling breathless
and her legs, too, seemed to be unaccountably weak
and trembling.

'Have you come with a message from Harry?' Beth
enquired eagerly. 'I know he's only been back in
England for a week, but it already seems such a long
time!' She laughed self-consciously. 'I know that it's
ridiculous, of course, but I was a little bit worried. I
mean, Harry said he was going to tell his family all

about our plans to get married, and I did wonder how his mother would react to an American daughter-in-law. Still, if you're here, everything must be all right!'

Oh Lord! thought Lorna swiftly, Beth obviously didn't yet realise that Alex wasn't here to spread good tidings of peace and joy to all mankind. She must try and get her sister out of the room for a quick and urgent warning.

'Of course both—er—Alex and I are dying to hear all your news, Beth. But how about coming to give me a hand in the kitchen, first.' She turned to smile brilliantly at the tall Englishman. 'I'm sure you'd like a cup of coffee, wouldn't you?'

'There's really no need . . .'

'But of course—I insist! Really, I haven't been entertaining you at all properly. What can you be thinking of me?'

What Alex was thinking, was only too obvious. From the sharp, piercing glance he sent in her direction, it was clear that he realised he was being temporarily outmanoeuvred; a state of affairs he didn't relish one bit if the hardening lines of his tanned face were anything to go by.

'We won't be a moment,' Lorna promised him with another false, beaming smile as she issued Beth out of the room.

'Don't you think he'd prefer a drink? I'm sure . . .'

'To hell with him!' Lorna snorted angrily, shutting the kitchen door and plugging in the coffee percolator before turning to face her sister. 'Now, Beth, we haven't much time. What in the hell has been going on while I've been away? And who exactly is Harry?'

'Harry? Harry Kendall is English—but of course you already know that! He was over here working for a firm on Wall Street: gaining a bit of experience about money and interest rates, he said. Anyway, he's gone back to England now, and wants me to come over for a visit to his home at Easter.' She grinned. 'Honestly, he never said anything about being related to a Lord, and I never connected the two names. Oh Lorna—Harry's wonderful, he really is. I—we're desperately in love, and I'm so happy I—I could cry!'

Lorna looked at her young sister, whose face was radiant with joy and happiness. As different from each other as chalk from cheese, Beth's colouring came from their mother's side of the family. Soft auburn curls surrounded her heart-shaped face, the large grey-blue eyes being her best feature especially when, as now, they sparkled with excitement. Much smaller than Lorna, who stood five foot ten in her stockinged feet, Beth's petite, softly curved slim figure was clothed in a simple grey dress. It had the effect of making her look fragile and almost ethereal.

How could Alex Kendall fail to see what a sweet, lovely girl Beth was? As for the unknown Harry—it was no surprise that he should have been drawn to her sister's gentle, warm personality. 'Have you known him long?' Lorna asked quietly.

'Only for about three months, but we both know that it's the real thing. It was quite extraordinary how we met. I mean, I didn't want to go to that stuffy party, but just when I thought I'd had enough and it was about time that I went home, Mrs van der Hoorst introduced me to Harry—and that was that!'

'And he really wants to marry you?'

'Of course he does!'

'Don't you think you're just a little young? I don't want you to be hurt, Beth . . .'

'For heaven's sake!' Beth laughed. 'I am twenty-one, you know! And anyway, you were only twenty when you ran off with Carlo Romani. You can't pretend that you weren't both terribly happy until . . .'

Lorna turned away to take the coffee cups down from the shelf. Why was it that after all these years, mention of his name could still cause her to catch her breath?

'Oh God, I'm sorry!' Beth came over to put an arm about her waist. 'I didn't mean to hurt you. It's just that I *know* Harry and I are right for each other, I really do.'

'You didn't hurt me, and anyway it all happened so long ago,' Lorna answered briskly, putting the coffee jug on the tray. 'However, while I'm happy for your good news, Beth, the bad news is sitting in the living room waiting for his coffee, I'm afraid.'

'You don't mean Alex, surely?

'Yup,' Lorna sighed. 'I don't think that I really understood what he was talking about—in fact I'm sure I didn't—and I certainly don't want to say anything that might make the issue more complicated than it is already. However, I think you'd better be prepared to find that Alex and his family are not exactly thrilled to hear about you and Harry getting married.'

'Why? What did he say?' Beth demanded urgently.

'Who cares what that awful man said? If you really and truly love each other, nothing else matters, surely?'

'Don't you like Alex?' Beth looked at her in astonishment. 'I mean—well, even if you had only just met each other, you were both—er—in a pretty tight clinch when I got home. Or was that just a figment of my imagination?' She smiled quizzically at her sister.

Lorna could feel her cheeks flushing with embarrassment. Really, at her age it was too ridiculous to mind what anyone thought, let alone her own sister. As for standing here and blushing like a schoolgirl ... 'Never mind that,' she said hurriedly, picking up the tray. 'I'll have to leave you to make up your own mind about *dear* Alex. Come on, let's go and beard the lion in our den, hmm?'

'Here we are!' she trilled nervously as she and Beth

returned to the living room. 'I do hope you haven't minded waiting for your coffee?'

'No, not at all,' he murmured smoothly, returning her beaming smile with an equally false one of his own.

Lorna found the sight less than reassuring. Oh-oh, she warned herself. His lordship had clearly had time to think while she and Beth were talking in the kitchen, and it very much looked as if he had decided to change his tactics. She suddenly remembered her father's maxim: that attack was the best form of defence.

'Beth's just been telling me about Harry. I've been abroad for almost a month, and so it's all come as a huge surprise. Wonderful, isn't it?' Once again she flashed him a brilliant smile.

'I wouldn't say "wonderful" was exactly the adjective I had in mind,' he drawled, taking up his cup and sipping the coffee. 'Possibly something along the lines of "an unfortunate mistake" might be more accurate.' He turned to Beth who was staring at him, the blood draining from her face. 'I'm very sorry, and I hope you will understand that my family's objections to your marriage have nothing to do with you personally. It's just that we have other plans for Harry, you see.'

'No, I don't see,' Lorna cut in angrily, 'and I'm damn sure that Beth doesn't either! If she and her Harry want to get married, why in the hell shouldn't they?

'Because Harry is already engaged to a very nice, suitable girl back in England, that's why!' he snapped. 'Why don't you mind your own business?'

'Beth's my sister,' Lorna retorted sharply. 'So her business is also my business. But I fail to see what interest you can have in this matter.'

Alex's hard mouth tightened as he visibly strove to keep his temper. 'I'm sorry to have to be the one to tell you,' he said gently to Beth, 'but it really won't do at all. Harry only came over to America because his family thought that he was too young to get married.

As you know, he's only twenty-two, and we felt he needed a greater experience of life before he settled down to marriage with Lavinia. Maybe he didn't tell you, but they were childhood sweethearts; and it has been understood for some time that they would marry as soon as Harry assumed his responsibilities on the estate. If he hadn't come over here, he wouldn't have met you, and would have settled down to a happily married life with Lavinia.'

Lorna glanced quickly at Beth, who looked stricken. Her facial colouring, normally a pale version of Lorna's, now looked completely drained, her skin a fine translucent veil stretched tightly over high cheekbones. She was clearly incapable of speech, staring down at her hands, her mouth quivering as if she would burst into tears at any moment. Couldn't the damn man see what he was doing to her sister?

'That's a very touching little story you've just given us,' she told him scathingly. 'However, it's clear to me, at least, that Harry must be seriously in love with Beth, otherwise the family wouldn't have pulled out their big guns and sent you over here. Right?'

'Wrong!' he retorted tersely. 'I'm having a retrospective exhibition at the Museum of Modern Art at the moment, and the family merely asked me to call and explain the position to Beth.'

'It still sounds to me as if Harry means business. And what can any of you do about it, anyway?'

'Oh God!' Alex groaned, running a distracted hand through his dark hair. 'I knew I shouldn't have agreed to come here. The plain fact is that Beth will be more or less a stranger in England, and if Harry's family don't approve or accept her, then her life could turn out to be fairly intolerable. Surely you can see that?'

With a strangled cry, Beth leapt to her feet and fled from the room, slamming the door loudly behind her.

Jumping up in consternation, Lorna hesitated for a

moment before turning furiously to face Alex. 'All I can see is that you've deeply hurt my poor sister,' she said bitterly. 'You had the nerve to tell me to mind my own business, so let's hear good and loud, just what it's all got to do with you?'

'But I've already told you that Harry is my heir.'

'So what?'

'Oh, for God's sake!' his voice rose in exasperation. 'How do I get it through your thick skull? If I die, Harry will inherit the title. Now do you understand?'

'My thick skull, as you so rudely put it, is quite capable of understanding that your imminent demise would be a great help to all concerned!' she told him angrily. 'Especially since it would prevent you from coming into someone's home and shouting at them!'

'I'm sorry—I apologise . . .'

'So I should damn well hope! It's hardly the behaviour one expects from a member of the English aristocracy, is it?' she queried, piling on the agony and noting his angry, flushed face with satisfaction.

'I've already said that I'm sorry . . .'

'Yes, I heard you. So let's cool this whole business down, shall we?' She waited to see whether he had any further insults to offer, and when he remained silent she took a deep breath to steady her nerves. If she was going to be of any help to Beth, she must try and find out exactly what the position was as far as Alex's family were concerned.

'OK, let's take it from the top.' Lorna continued. 'As I understand it, you are not married and Harry is due to inherit your title when you die—right so far?'

'Quite correct,' he murmured, relaxing back in his chair.

'Exactly what relationship is Harry to you?'

'Harry Kendall is my first cousin,' Alex explained in a calmer tone of voice. 'His father and mine were brothers. They are both dead now, and while my mother has married again, Harry's mother remains a widow, living at present in my family home in Oxfordshire with the twins—Harry's brother and sister, who are younger than him, of course.'

'OK, I get it now. Aunt Sophie is Harry's mother, I assume?' As he nodded, Lorna looked at him speculatively. 'Now, I wonder why you and your family should be all so steamed up about Harry falling in love with Beth?' she mused slowly. 'As you say, the boy is young and you might well have expected him to sow a lot of wild oats before he settled down—especially if he followed your example!' She couldn't resist the pointed jibe, but to her surprise he gave a dry bark of laughter.

'*Touché!*' He smiled at her with wry amusement.

'All right. So here we have this nice old English family apparently worried sick that Harry has quite clearly fallen out of love with Lavinia—whoever she is—and slap bang into love with Beth. My sister, by the way, is a very talented musician, and if you think I'm happy about the possibility of her giving up her piano studies to marry your cousin, you can think again!'

A cynical smile twisted his lips. 'So why don't *you* try and talk her out of this infatuation?'

'We'll leave me out of it, for the moment. I'm far more interested in finding out exactly what you have against my sister,' she demanded trenchantly. 'She's a very pretty girl, with a sweet character—and besides, you'd already made up your mind she wouldn't do before you ever saw her. Now why?'

'All this is pointless speculation,' he drawled dismissively. 'You can just take it from me, certainly as far as my mother and aunt are concerned, that Harry's romance with your sister is totally unacceptable.'

Gazing at his impassive face, the heavy lids lowered to hide all expression in his eyes; wild, speculative thoughts raced through Lorna's brain. 'It's—it's to do with money, isn't it?' she suddenly exclaimed. 'Of course—that's it! Old family, down on its beam ends, suddenly rescued by a rich wife for Harry ... Oh boy! I can see it all now. I just bet Lavinia's old dad is full of juice—where does it come from, oil or steel?'

Alex's blue eyes hardened for a moment, before he shrugged his broad shoulders, smiling sardonically as she glared so furiously at him from across the room. 'I believe it's soap powder, actually,' he drawled.

'My God!' Lorna was suddenly swept by a tide of fury. 'You're just the sort of guy who would sell his own grandmother to bet on a horse race! You make a big deal about your so-called title, and yet you don't give a damn about your poor cousin. I notice that you have no intention of marrying to oblige your family, so why in the hell should he?'

'You don't understand,' he retorted. 'It isn't me you have to convince, it's the rest of the family.'

'Oh yes?' Lorna snorted in disbelief. 'Well, I hope Harry has the spunk to stand up to you all. As far as I'm concerned, he and Beth can get married tomorrow if they want to—don't forget that they are both free, white and over twenty-one!'

Strangely, Alex didn't seem particularly worried or upset as her defiant words rang around the room. Rising from his chair, he walked slowly over to stand looking down into her gold-flecked green eyes, which were sparkling with anger. 'The battle lines would seem to have been drawn up,' he murmured. 'That, I take it, is your final word on the subject?'

'No, not quite! You apparently aren't worried about having double standards, but maybe the next time you settle down to one of your practised flirtations, or a little light seduction, you might have the grace to feel ashamed of what you've said and done to my sister today!'

Infuriatingly, his only response to her caustic words was a long, lazy smile. 'Why don't you join me for dinner tomorrow, and we can then discuss the whole business in more relaxed surroundings, hmm?'

Gazing back at him in astonishment, Lorna could feel her heart thumping wildly, her senses assaulted by his sensual charm. As soon as she'd set eyes on him, she had realised that he was trouble with a capital 'T'. And despite knowing that, and also what a swine he had been to Beth, she could still feel herself going weak at the knees beneath the force of his smile. The man was a damn menace!

'You—you must be out of your mind!' she snapped. 'I wouldn't be seen dead with you—not if you were the last man on earth. Forget it!'

'What a charming refusal!' he murmured, one dark eyebrow raised in amusement. Before she realised what he was doing, he caught hold of her hand and lifted it to his lips.

'OK—that's it. You've had your fun for tonight!' she hissed, her face flaming as she snatched her hand away and went swiftly over to the door. 'You've got exactly five seconds to leave this apartment before I call for the security guards, and anyone else I can think of.'

'Don't forget the police and the fire service while you're about it!' he laughed, swiftly lowering his head to brush his mouth across her lips before he stode towards the front door.

'Get lost . . .!' she shouted furiously, slamming the door behind his departing figure, leaving only the sound of his mocking laughter to ring in her ears.

Later that night as Lorna lay restlessly tossing and turning in her bed, the events of the day kept running through her tired brain. What on earth could she do to help Beth? Hurrying into her sister's room after Alex left, she had found Beth lying across her bed and sobbing as if her heart were broken.

'Oh, darling, don't cry. Everything's going to be all

right,' she murmured softly, leaning over and putting an arm about the young girl's trembling figure.

'I'm—I'm s-sorry to be so s-silly,' Beth stuttered, sobs still shaking her body as she sat up and gazed at Lorna with eyes that were blinded by tears.

'You're not being silly—it's a perfectly normal reaction,' Lorna said firmly, reaching for a box of tissues and gently wiping away the tears. 'But I do think we must start being practical, don't you? It doesn't mean the end of the world if Harry's family don't approve of your engagement, despite what that foul Alex said! That's the first thing to remember. After all, his family don't even know you, so it's just the *idea* they seem to be worried about—right?'

'But what can I possibly do? I mean . . .' Beth sniffed unhappily.

'I don't know at the moment, but I'll definitely think of something. So don't worry, OK?'

Beth gave a shaky laugh. 'That's what you always used to say when I was small!'

Lorna smiled at her sister. 'Well, I was right then, so you can take it that my magic formula will succeed again!' Looking at Beth's small, pale and tear-stained face, the blue-grey eyes glazed with misery as she bravely tried to smile, Lorna found herself wishing that Alex Kendall was still in the apartment. It would have given her the greatest possible pleasure to thump him on the nose for what he had done to her sister.

'What we both need is a stiff drink and some food,' she said decisively. 'So while I'm fixing supper, why don't you have a nice hot bath and then you can tell me all about it, hmm?'

'Oh, that's better,' Lorna said, putting down her fork half an hour later. 'I hadn't realised I was so hungry.' She looked across the pine kitchen table at Beth who had eaten no more than a few mouthfuls of her omelette, gazing despondently down as she absentmindedly pushed the food around her plate. With a small sigh Lorna stood up, silently removing the dishes and placing a cup of coffee in front of her sister. 'Do you feel like talking now?' she asked gently.

'I—I don't know where to start . . .' Beth muttered.

'Well, how about at the beginning? You say you met your Harry at some party—then what happened?'

'Well, it was very crowded, and I was just about to leave, when I was introduced to him. It was—it was quite extraordinary! I mean, all that business I'd read about in romantic novels, how the heroine meets someone for the first time and pow! they're in love—I always thought it was rubbish.' She looked pleadingly at her sister. 'I don't know if you can understand, but that's exactly what happened, it really did!'

'I've had my moments too, you know!' Lorna murmured dryly, but she did know exactly what Beth meant. That was how she had felt when she had first met Carlo. An instantaneous feeling of total rapport, the dizzy, mind-shattering knowledge that this was *the* man. Remembering how it had been all those years ago, she had to make a determined effort to banish the painful recollections and concentrate on what Beth was saying.

'. . . so he took me out to dinner, to a lovely little restaurant. I honestly can't remember where it was or what we ate, the time just seemed to fly by as we talked and talked.' She gave a small, nervous grin. 'I expect you know what I mean.'

Lorna smiled wryly. 'More or less. Is that when he told you he was engaged to another girl?'

'No, not then. Not for some time, in fact.'

'And by the time he did, I suppose it was too late. For you, I mean,' Lorna added grimly.

'It—it wasn't really his fault,' Beth said, quickly on the defensive. 'First of all, the subject never came up. It never occurred to me, you see.' She sighed heavily.

'We'd been out with each other for some weeks, before he took me back to his apartment one evening, and told me all about it. I was upset, of course I was,' she assured Lorna earnestly. 'But when he said that he had sort of drifted into getting engaged to Lavinia, more or less because it was expected by his family, and that now he was desperately in love with me and wanted us to get married . . .' She gave an unhappy shrug.

'He does sound awfully young,' Lorna murmured. She couldn't help thinking that if Harry could be pushed by his family into getting engaged to someone he didn't love, he must be pretty spineless and definitely not a good prospect for Beth. However, this wasn't the moment to say so.

'He's almost two years older than me—he'll be twenty-three next month,' Beth said quickly.

'Really ancient!' Lorna grinned, prompting a reluctant smile from her sister.

'Well, I know it was wrong, but I sort of forgot about his English fiancée,' Beth continued. 'I mean, I was so totally in love with him by then, and it was clear that he didn't *feel* anything for the other girl.' She looked up and caught Lorna's eye. 'He really does love me, you know,' she said with a slight flush. 'He had to return to England last week, and he phoned three nights ago to say that he had told his mother we were going to get married. He never said a word about the family not approving.'

'What about—er—Lavinia?'

'Well, that's what I really don't understand!' Beth burst out. 'Harry assured me that he had spoken to her, and he was terribly relieved to find that she didn't want to get married any more than he did. I rather gathered from him that her father is a bit of an ogre, and now she feels she can stand up to him and do her own thing.'

'Which is . . .?' Lorna queried.

'I'm not really sure,' Beth shrugged. 'Something to do

with designing clothes, I think. Anyway, that's why I was so shocked and upset by Alex Kendall. I'm certain as I can be that Harry's telling the truth, and yet why should his cousin come here and say that the family don't approve?'

'Yes, it does sound as if everyone has rather gone into a tail-spin, doesn't it?' Lorna mused quietly. 'However, I did have some words with Alex after you left the room, and I gather that Lavinia's father is very wealthy. I'm almost sure, especially since Alex didn't contradict me, that the family had been hoping for some of the girl's money to come their way.' She laughed ruefully. 'It sounds positively like the story of the Duke of Marlborough marrying the Vanderbilt heiress—only that happened almost a hundred years ago, not in the nineteen-eighties, for heaven's sake!

'But what am I going to do now?' Beth moaned.

It was just the same as when they were children and Beth had come running to her for help. Although she knew she ought to let her sister sort out her own difficulties, the habits of a lifetime were too well ingrained, Lorna realised, for her to do anything other than try and solve Beth's problem.

'I don't think you should do anything at the moment,' she said slowly. 'After all, it's now up to Harry, isn't it? I know it's not going to be easy for you, but if and when he phones again, then I think you can ask him what's going on. Didn't you say he'd invited you to go and stay with his family for Easter? Well then,' she said as Beth nodded, 'the ball is firmly in your Harry's court.'

'But I couldn't possibly go over there on my own!' Beth gasped in horror. 'Not knowing how they feel about me.'

'Of course you can. Harry's the only one who matters, surely?'

'Oh, Lorna, can't you come with me?'

'Not a chance!' Lorna shook her head, smiling ruefully in response to her sister's plea. 'I'm sorry, darling, but I'm sure that I'm booked up solid, and goodness knows what Mercy Bird has lined up for me while I've been away. You'll be fine on your own, you'll see.' She glanced down at her wrist. 'It's getting late and you've got your music classes tomorrow, so it's time we both went to bed.' She rose from the table and went over to give Beth a hug. 'Don't worry, darling. I'm sure that everything will be all right.'

Now, as she lay in bed, Lorna could only wish that she believed in her own confident words. Unfortunately, she very much feared that the pressure from Harry's family would prove too much for him. The thoughts about how she could best try and help her sister if the worst happened, chased round and round her tired brain, and it wasn't until some hours later that she at last fell into a heavy sleep.

It seemed only minutes later that she was dragged to the surface of consciousness by the ringing of the phone beside her bed. With her eyes still shut, she flailed helplessly around until her hand came into contact with the receiver.

'Lorna? Lorna Grant?'

'Y-yes, who—who is it . . .' she mumbled, still half asleep.

'Alex Kendall here.'

'W-what . . .!' Lorna struggled to sit up, putting on the bedside light and looking groggily at her small alarm clock. 'Do—do you know what time it is?' she groaned. 'It's only seven o'clock, for God's sake!'

Alex's lazy, amused chuckle rang in her ear. 'How can you possibly be still asleep on such a lovely spring morning?'

'Very easily!' she muttered. 'What do you want?'

'You, of course! But until that happy day arrives—if

you cannot join me for dinner tonight, how about lunch, hmm?'

He hadn't really said . . . He didn't mean . . . No, of course not! It was just her overheated imagination, she told herself, suddenly feeling wide awake. Why on earth should he want to see her again? He must be hoping to get her to change her mind about Beth and Harry . . .

'Hello—are you still there?' His words cut into her reverie.

'Yes, and the answer is "no".'

'No . . .?'

'No, I won't have lunch with you.'

'I'm really very nice when you get to know me!'

Lorna steeled herself against the dark, husky tones, which even down the telephone wire had the effect of making her toes curl. 'Yes, I can remember reading about just how nice you are—Merle Forest's "Kiss and tell all" story in the newspapers was very explicit!' she retorted dryly. 'Not to mention some of your other ladies, such as Tiffany Wild and that floozie, Rita Valentine, who always seems to lose the top of her bikini just as soon as a photographer comes into sight!'

'Hang on,' he protested. 'Rita's a nice girl, a real homebody.'

'From what I've seen of her body—it isn't kept at home very often!' she snapped.

'Ouch! Well, that's disposed of poor Rita,' he laughed softly. 'So, if you won't have lunch or dinner, can I persuade you to come and look at my photographs in the exhibition?'

She could feel herself weakening at the seductive tone of his voice, and if she didn't get off the phone soon, God knows what she'd find herself agreeing to! 'You're certainly persistent, I'll say that for you. However, I'm afraid the answer to all your kind invitations is thanks—but no thanks. 'Bye.'

Lorna was irritated to see that her hand was trembling as she replaced the receiver. That well-known Casanova, Alex Kendall, should be fed strong sedatives and kept firmly locked away behind bars in a cage. Just look how he was affecting her—and she didn't even *like* the damned man, for heaven's sake!

CHAPTER THREE

LATER that morning as Lorna entered the huge modern skyscraper that housed the Beautiful Birds Agency, she tried to think why Mercy Bird should have been so insistent that Lorna dropped all her plans for the day, and came in to see her as soon as possible. 'I've got something to discuss with you, honey, but I haven't the time to go into it all now. So, just get yourself over here, and we can have a good long talk, OK?' Lorna couldn't extract any further details from Mercy, who had sounded unusually animated and not at all her normal tough, prosaic self. Still mystified, Lorna left the elevator and walked through the crowded glass-and-chrome offices.

Mercy's secretary stopped typing and smiled at her approach. 'Here, I'll take that,' she murmured as Lorna shrugged off her black raincoat, which was damp from the steady downpour outside.

'Thanks Sharon. Heavens—what a day!'

'Mrs Bird said that you were to go straight in when you arrived,' Sharon said, carefully slipping the wet coat on to a hanger, her hands relishing the soft, sensuous texture of its mink lining. With a small, inward sigh she turned back to view Lorna shaking the drops of rain from her long blonde hair. It was no good. Never, in a million years, would she be able to look so coolly elegant as the tall girl clothed in a fluid pale grey suit made of the finest suede, a white silk shirt tied in a large, floppy bow at her neck. 'Would you like some coffee?' she added.

'Yes, please. You'd better make it black—I've got a feeling I'm going to need it!'

Sharon laughed. 'The boss lady isn't at all dragon-like this morning, you'll be pleased to hear!' A statement borne out by the beaming smile with which Mercy greeted Lorna's arrival in her office.

'Come right in, honey. How were the Paris Collections? The usual terrible confusion, I expect?'

Lorna sank down into a comfortable chair. 'You're so right! It's always a madhouse.'

'Donald Roberts, one of the photographers for *Women's Wear Daily*, called in yesterday on his way back from Paris.' Mercy gave her a wintry smile. 'He told me that he used to be a war photographer, until it all got too much for him and he changed to fashion work. However, he now thinks that maybe he should return to his old job. After all the razzamatazz of the Paris Collections, he reckons that working in the Lebanon would be a whole lot more peaceful!'

They were both laughing as Mercy's secretary entered with two cups of coffee. 'Please cancel all my calls for the next hour, Sharon,' Mercy said, her tiny, bright blue eyes sweeping over the girl's figure. 'Your skirt looks a little tight, dear,' she added. 'Maybe you should go on a diet, hmm?'

'Yes, Mrs Bird,' Sharon murmured meekly, turning away to wink at Lorna before shutting the door quietly behind her.

Mercy turned to gaze at the slim girl who was sitting in front of her and quietly sipping her coffee. 'That's a nice suit—Ralph Lauren? Well,' she continued as Lorna nodded, 'I'm sorry to say that you're not doing it justice. You look positively haggard this morning.'

'I know!' Lorna groaned. 'I didn't sleep very well last night, and then—wouldn't you know it!—a crazy man woke me up with a 'phone call at the crack of dawn.'

'Well, dear, I'm sure I don't have to mention the importance of keeping yourself looking fresh and wide-awake, do I? I told you, the last time you were in the office, that you weren't getting any younger.'

'Yes, I know,' Lorna muttered, feeling depressed at the rasping, warning note in Mercy's voice. Had her agent called her in today to tell her that her career as a top fashion model was over? If so, what on earth was she to do? The main purpose of her life for the last three years, the need to support Beth and to pay for her musical education, would soon be coming to an end. She had accumulated sufficient funds to support Beth in the future, since it would be a long time before her sister was sufficiently well-known to earn enough to live on; the road for a concert pianist was known to be a hard and stony one. Of course, there was now the uncertainty about Beth's engagement to Harry. Despite her defiant words to Alex last night, she very much feared that the love affair wouldn't have a happy ending—not with all his family opposed to the idea. Really, why couldn't Alex Kendall just mind his own business, and keep his nose out of the affair?

Lorna took a deep breath, resolutely closing her mind to the memory of Alex's disturbing personality and tried to concentrate her thoughts on her own future. What was she, herself, going to do . . .?

'We must think about your future.' Mercy's voice cut into her reverie, accurately echoing her own dismal thoughts. 'You've still got a few years at the top, of course. But we must decide what you're going to do after that, and begin planning it right away.'

'I'm relieved to hear that you think I've still got a bit of mileage left! However, as to how I'm going to earn my living when I'm an old hag of thirty—I haven't a clue, I'm afraid.' Lorna shrugged her slim shoulders. 'I'm really not interested in designing clothes under my own label, like so many other ex-models that I know. I can't even draw a straight line, for heaven's sake!' She grinned at Mercy, who was frowning impatiently and drumming her fingers on the desk.

'None of my girls seem to listen to a word I say!'

'Oh, come on, Mercy! Who do you think you're fooling—you know very well that they're all terrified of you!'

'So I should damn well hope!' Mercy growled, frowning as Lorna shook with laughter. She had long ago discovered the warmth and kindness, normally well hidden beneath her agent's outwardly tough, aggressive personality.

'When I said *we* must decide what you're going to do in the future—I was referring to you and I,' Mercy said firmly. 'No one is indispensable, no one can go on forever, and I've got my old age to think of as well, you know.'

Lorna looked at the older woman in surprise. Mercy Bird had been a well-known New York character as long as she could remember, and Lorna's obvious first choice of an agent when she had decided to take the plunge into freelance work. Until this moment, it had never occurred to her that Mercy could be contemplating her retirement from the Agency; a business she had founded and run for many years. Gazing with sudden dismay into the bright blue eyes, set in a face whose skin was creased and lined like tanned leather, Lorna thought that Mercy looked as she had always done— tough and indestructible.

'There's no need to look so shocked—I'm not intending to turn my toes up just yet! However, it's only sensible to think ahead, as I'm sure you'll agree.' Mercy turned in her swivel chair to look out of the window. 'This is a tough town, you know. So many agencies scrabbling for the top jobs—I used to say that I had a crick in my neck, just from trying to keep an eye on the knives poised behind my back!' She gave a dry laugh and spun her chair back to face Lorna. 'Don't get me wrong, I've loved every damn, conniving minute! But now, well, I guess I'm getting just a little tired of it all. It's time to let someone else have a go. Besides, I've become really very fond of you Lorna, especially since you are one of the few girls on my books who's never given me any hassle!'

'You—you can't be thinking of—of me?' Lorna gasped. 'Really, I . . . It's simply not my scene. I'd be hopeless at all the in-fighting, and . . .'

'Relax, kiddo!' Mercy laughed. 'Give me enough credit to know that it's not the sort of job to suit you. No, I've got a much better idea—one that I've been thinking about for some time. How about you and me forming a partnership and setting up one of those Keep Fit places, hmm?'

'A what . . .?' Lorna looked at her in some confusion. Whatever she had thought Mercy was going to say this morning, this certainly wasn't it!

'Well, what I had in mind was something on the lines of an exclusive club. Somewhere with a glamorous swimmimg pool, jacuzzis, saunas, steam rooms and lots of different kinds of massage. But not only that, of course,' Mercy added, 'we would also offer various beauty treatments, and maybe acupuncture and osteopathy as well, which would naturally mean having a doctor and nurse on the premises. What do you think, hmm?'

Lorna's brain was whirling. 'I—I really don't know what I think. The idea sounds great fun and it might work, although I'm sure that there are already quite a few places like that, which have been established for some time.'

'Yes, I know. But this would be a really top-notch, up-market project. We'd have a large building, with a first-class restaurant, champagne bar and all that jazz. What's more, it would be open to men as well as women, and we'd make the annual membership fee simply *astronomical*!' Mercy grinned wolfishly. 'That'll be sure to pull them in!'

'I really don't see ...' Lorna shook her head in bemusement.

'Look kiddo,' Mercy rasped. 'Anyone who is anyone in this town is a damn snob—right? If we make this place so exclusive that the members will have to be either multi-millionaires, or their ancestors came over here with the Mayflower, people will be falling over themselves to apply. Believe me—it can't fail!'

'And—and you want me to be your partner?'

'With your looks and your name for publicity, together with my business know-how—I guarantee that we'll have a smash hit on our hands.'

Lorna sat back in her chair, the remains of her coffee growing cold as she thought about the proposition. Mercy was certainly no fool, and if she thought that the scheme was a viable one ... 'What about the finance?' she asked.

'I thought we'd carve it straight down the middle, half each.' Mercy said, mentioning a sum of money needed to start the project that made Lorna gasp. 'Now come on, kiddo. Since I take ten per cent, I obviously know exactly what you've been earning, and it sure isn't peanuts! I also reckon you've been a shrewd girl and will have salted some of your money away against a rainy day, right?'

'Well, yes—but this is going to take just about all that I've managed to save. I must admit that I'm tempted by the idea ...' Lorna sighed. 'However, I've got to consider my sister's future as well as my own.'

'Oh, God, look at the time!' Mercy consulted her wristwatch. 'I've got a whole lot of people waiting to see me. All I'm suggesting at the moment is that you think about the idea, OK?'

'I'll certainly do that,' Lorna assured her as she left the office. She was so immersed in her thoughts that she walked blindly past the crowd of hopeful, beautiful young girls waiting to be interviewed by Mercy. Nervously clutching their large portfolios full of photographs, their wistful, envious glances followed her well-known figure as they promised themselves that they, too, would one day realise their dreams of being a top model and every bit as rich and famous as Lorna Grant.

She left the building and hailed a cab, leaning back in the seat as her dazed mind tried to grapple with all the ramifications of her meeting with Mercy. It was some moments before she realised that the cab had stopped, and the driver was impatiently trying to attract her attention.

'Wake up, lady. We've arrived and I sure can't sit here all day!'

'Here . . .?' Lorna looked around in confusion. 'What—what am I doing here?'

'How in the hell do I know?' The cab driver shrugged his shoulders, sighing with exasperation. 'The Museum of Modern Art was what you said—and the Museum of Modern Art is where we're at, OK? Of course, I could be wrong. God knows, I've only been driving a cab in this town for twenty years . . .'

'No, I—I'm sorry, I . . .' Lorna flushed at the rough sarcasm in his voice and hurriedly got out, pushing some dollar bills into his outstretched hand. *'Women!'* she heard him snort as he drove away, leaving her standing uncertainly outside the large building.

Why on earth had she told the cab driver to bring her to such a place? She didn't even particularly like modern paintings, for heaven's sake! And—and it certainly hadn't been her intention to take up Alex's invitation to view his photographic exhibition—one which was bound to consist mainly of pictures of sexy women! Hesitating, she shrugged helplessly and moments later found herself automatically paying the entrance money as she cudgelled her brains, desperately trying to account for her presence in the museum. It wasn't as if she had even bothered to think about Alex—not after his phone call this morning. Well, maybe that wasn't strictly true, she thought, feeling cross and annoyed with herself. Still, since for some quite inexplicable reason she was here, she supposed she might as well look around . . .

It was years since she'd last visited the museum. Not since her father had brought her here at the age of thirteen, she remembered, moving slowly through the large rooms. She recalled how disappointed he had been at her lack of interest in contemporary art, and was suddenly swept by a fierce pang of poignant regret, wishing that he was still alive today so that she could tell him of her delight in some of the paintings on view. Not that she cared for them all, of course, but she had been quite overcome by the haunting, mystical beauty of Andrew Wyeth's pictures. Particularly those depicting the old houses and countryside of Maine, which took her immediately back in time to the idyllically happy summer vacations she and Beth had spent at the family house on Monhegan Island.

'He's an outstanding painter, isn't he?'

The rich, dark tones of the voice cutting into the silence made Lorna jump with shock, her long gold hair flying about her shoulders as she whirled to see Alex leaning nonchalantly against the far wall.

'You gave me a f-fright. What—what are you d-doing here?' she stammered, instantly regretting the stupid question as she felt her face redden beneath the cool, blue eyes which gleamed with cynical amusement.

'Well, I do have some photographs on display downstairs, you know!' he murmured. 'However, I've just been having a few words with a member of the staff here, and also taking another look at Monet's *Water Lilies*—quite one of my favourite paintings. Since we're on the subject—what, may I ask, are *you* doing here? I seem to remember a quite definite—er—refusal to my invitation this morning!'

'I was just passing,' she said airily, hoping that she didn't sound quite as idiotic as she felt.

'Really?' he commented dryly, his dark brows lifting in sardonic, mocking disbelief.

'I—um ...' She glanced up through her eyelashes into his face, and then turned quickly away as she noticed his mouth twitching with amusement. The damn man was laughing at her! Gazing blindly at a picture on the wall, she desperately cast about in her mind for inspiration. How could she possibly explain her unexpected appearance in this building, when she didn't even know why she had come, either?

'Are you really such an admirer of that particular artist?'

'What—what do you mean ...?' Lorna jerked her head sideways, startled to find that Alex's tall, broad-shouldered figure was now standing close beside her. Following his eyes, she saw that she had been staring at a canvas completely covered in a thoroughly nasty shade of sick green, criss-crossed by what looked like muddy bicycle tyre marks. 'Ugh—how horrible!' she thought, before realising from Alex's laughter that she must have spoken aloud.

'Quite right,' he agreed. 'I can promise you that my pictures are much better!'

'I can guess *just* what they're like!' she muttered crossly. His piercing blue eyes were gazing at her intently and she felt herself beginning to feel even more flustered than she was already, if that were possible. Her face flamed with embarrassment. So what if she couldn't think of a good excuse for being here? There was absolutely no reason for her to feel so—well, so sort of guilty, almost as if she had been caught spying. Did he think that she'd sneaked in here to see his exhibition on the quiet? Well, the arrogant man could just have another thought—because she hadn't even seen his damn photographs! What's more, she wasn't the slightest bit interested in viewing pictures of movie starlets, and ...

'Come along,' he said, taking her hand and leading her out of the room and down the stairs. Too confused by his close proximity and the warmth of his firm grip, Lorna cursed herself, furious at not being able to think of a suitably crushing reply as he led her into a small room which was clearly set aside for temporary exhibitions.

'Well?' Alex murmured some minutes later, watching as she wandered slowly and thoughtfully from one photograph to another. 'As someone who must have been photographed by all the top names, I'd be interested to know what you think?'

'They—they're not ...'

'... not what you were expecting to see?' He gave a dry bark of laughter. 'My dear girl, I'd get suffocatingly bored if I had to do nothing else but take portraits—however interesting the subject.'

Lorna found herself regarding Alex with an increasing, if grudging, respect. Of course there were portraits in the exhibition, but they mostly consisted of elderly European statesmen, although she noted that he had included some eminent Americans, including Presidents Carter and Reagan.

The main group of pictures, however, seemed to have been taken over a period of approximately ten years. Both in black and white and colour, the photographs revealed an Englishman's discovery and appreciation of rural America: the school bus; county jails with their inhabitants—on both sides of the law; small farmers and their families working the land; the lonely cowhand with his cattle on the deserted prairie; the men gathered in the saloon and women gossiping together at the local grocery store.

'Well?' Alex repeated.

'You don't need me to tell you that they're good—really excellent,' Lorna said over her shoulder, turning back to look at a separate group of pictures. 'But these—these are awful! Not the photography itself,' she added quickly. 'I mean that the subject is so—so ...' She shook her head, momentarily unable to express her feelings.

'Man's inhumanity to man,' Alex said softly, coming over to stand beside her as she gazed at the terrible, heart-rending pictures of refugees who had fled from the Russian presence in Afghanistan. Starving children clung weakly to their equally emaciated mothers, while the men, wearing only rags, grimly carried their family's few, precious possessions.

'I was in Pakistan last year,' he continued, 'and by chance I heard that a group of people had managed to escape over the mountain passes. I hurried up to one of the camps to find that they were just arriving. They're an incredibly tough, fierce people, the Afghans. Just look at that old boy.' He pointed to an ancient, wizened old man who was shown shuffling along the dusty road, nearly bent double by the long roll of bedding that he was carrying.

'He looks so very frail,' Lorna murmured. 'Why didn't someone help him to carry that load?'

'Because for one thing he wouldn't have let them, and for another he's got his old rifle in that bundle—and he sure isn't going to let go of that! He may not have any ammunition, or indeed any food; but I can practically guarantee that his rifle would be in mint condition, and ready for use. In fact I know it was, because I returned some weeks later and heard that the old boy had grabbed some bullets from somewhere, and quickly hoofed it back over the border! Anyway, that's enough of that—we must hurry, or we'll be late for lunch.'

She looked up at him in baffled confusion. 'Lunch?'

'Of course. I'm starving, and you look as if you could do with a decent meal.'

'I don't think that I . . .'

'Of course you want to have lunch with me—that's why you're here. So let's stop wasting time.'

Lorna was furiously indignant as he took her arm in a firm grip, steering her across the hall and out on to the sidewalk. 'If—if you think that I came here just to have lunch with you, you must be out of your mind!' she hissed. 'It's no good you trying to argue about Beth and Harry . . .'

'Who said anything about Beth and Harry?' he demanded with a mocking smile as he waved down a passing cab. 'Let's face it, darling,' he murmured, opening the door and bundling her inside, 'we both know you couldn't resist my bright blue eyes!'

Lorna was speechless with anger as his peal of laughter rang around the enclosed space. 'My God! You've got a nerve—and don't you dare call me d-darling, either!' she spluttered. 'Never, in all my life, have I ever met anyone so pig-headed, so arrogant, so . . . so . . .'

'How about: handsome, charming and witty?' he asked with a grin. 'Calm down and relax, you gorgeous girl. I was only teasing!'

Lorna edged as far away from Alex as she could, wrathfully eyeing him sideways from beneath her lashes. The man was absolutely impossible! He seemed to have the quite extraordinary idea that he was irresistible to women. Well, so he might be, for some poor fools who couldn't see further than their own noses; but she wasn't one of them! OK, she was fully prepared to acknowledge, privately to herself, that he undoubtedly possessed enormous charm. She might even admit, if she was feeling especially charitable—which she certainly wasn't at the moment—that he was a very sexy gentleman.

Having said all that—so what? The world was full of charming men, but she didn't have to go out to lunch with one of them—not if she didn't want to. Which immediately raised the question of why she was in this cab? All she had to do was to tell the driver to pull over, and then get out and walk away. So, why wasn't she doing just that . . .?

Lorna's distracted thoughts were interrupted by their arrival outside a restaurant to which she had never been before.

'Well, are you going to join me for lunch? Or shall I get out and let you go on your way, hmm?'

Lorna glared indignantly at Alex's amused expression. What in the hell was she supposed to say now? A vehement 'no', or a simpering 'yes'? Temporarily lost for words and torn by indecision, she felt an overwhelming urge to slap the grin from his face.

'She who hesitates is lost,' he mocked, taking her arm and helping her dismount from the cab.

'I don't suppose they'll have a table available, anyway,' she muttered, casting a doubtful look at the rundown condition of the building.

'Oh yes, they will,' he replied with maddening certainty. 'And don't let the exterior put you off. The steaks here are a dream!'

Their arrival was greeted by the manager, fawning obsequiously as if Alex owned the place, Lorna thought sourly and, as they were bowed to a secluded table set apart from the other diners, she said as much.

'You're quite right, I do! It's one of the best investments I've ever made. I never have to worry about where to go for a meal, and I always get fantastic service!'

'Heads would roll if you didn't, you mean,' she snapped.

'Precisely! Now, you beauty, I can see that what you need is a good, strong drink, rapidly followed by a large, juicy steak. That should help to put you in a better mood, don't you think, hmm?'

Lorna was just about to vigorously protest that if she was in a bad mood, it was entirely his fault, when she saw the gleaming glint of laughter in his blue eyes. 'You are totally and utterly incorrigible!' she said, trying not to respond to his warm smile.

'Alas, how very true,' he agreed sorrowfully. 'I knew all along that you'd be an understanding girl—I'm sadly in need of tender, loving care, you know.'

'You're *what* . . .?' Lorna gasped, and then found herself collapsing with laughter. 'Oh boy, that's simply got to be the quote of the year!' she managed to say at last, wiping the tears of mirth from her eyes.

'That's better,' he said blandly, ordering two dry martinis from a hovering waiter, before turning back to Lorna. 'You're even more beautiful when you laugh.'

She could feel herself colouring slightly at the gleam in the vivid blue eyes slowly roaming over her face and figure. What was wrong with her, for heaven's sake? She wasn't a blushing teenager, but a fairly sophisticated woman of twenty-five, and well used in her modelling career to being looked at in that speculative manner. However, it was definitely about time that Alex was made to understand the facts of life—as far as she was concerned, anyway!

'Look, *loverboy*—I'd hate you to think that I don't admire your technique.' She gave him a saccharin-sweet smile. 'I mean, it's a very impressive *numero uno* production, OK? But I reckon it's now my turn to tell *you* to relax. I'm sure that you have a great line in chatting up us women, however, I can assure you that there's no need to roll out the charm on my account.' She smiled up at a waiter as he placed a large drink on the table before her.

'I am mortally wounded—cut to the quick! How could you possibly believe that I would ever indulge in such disgraceful behaviour. "Roll out the charm", indeed!' he gave a dramatic shudder as he passed her the menu.

Lorna laughed at his parody of an upper-class Englishman, awarding him alpha plus for taking the put-down so well. Apart from a slight tightening of his mouth at her words, there had been no discernible change in his facial expression. Waiting until a waiter had taken their order, she asked him how an English lord came to be a successful photographer.

'Oh, there's nothing remarkable about that,' he assured her, grinning ironically as he acknowledged the deliberate change of subject. 'There are lots of us aristos in the profession nowadays—it's practically become the accepted thing! There's Patrick Lichfield, Derry Moore, Charles Settrington and many more. Nobody really bothers whether you have a title or not, the only criteria is: Can the chap take a good photograph? If he can, he's in business; if he can't and is just fooling around, then no one is going to employ him. It's as simple as that.'

'How did you get started?' she queried, interested and intrigued, despite her strong disapproval of his personal lifestyle.

'I had a very boring but typical English upbringing. After coming down from university, I bummed around for a bit and then decided that since I'd always been mad keen on photography, it made sense to try and earn my living at the job. Eventually I found someone to take me on as that lowest of lowly worms, a photographic assistant.' He smiled and shrugged his shoulders. 'That's it, really. One thing led to another, I had a few lucky breaks, and here I am—actually having lunch with one of the world's top models! What more has life to hold for me?'

'According to the gossip columns—a few teeth knocked out by jealous husbands, if you don't soon mend your licentious ways!' Lorna said crisply, smiling broadly as he threw back his head and roared with laughter.

'What a marvellous girl you are!' he exclaimed, taking her hand and raising it to his lips. 'I'm falling more madly in love with you every minute!'

Lorna felt her stomach suddenly lurch, her breathing becoming ragged and uneven at the warm, caressing tone in his voice. Snatching back her hand as soon as he released it, she was thankfully rescued from the need to say anything by the arrival of the waiter with her steak à poivre. She suddenly realised, with a nasty jolt, that despite her words earlier, she was in imminent danger of succumbing to his overwhelming charm—just like all the other women in his life. Really, the man's personality was positively lethal!

'Apart from telling you not to believe all the trash you read in the gossip columns, I think that we have discussed me quite long enough,' Alex smiled. 'I'm far more interested in hearing about you.'

'Unlike yourself, I'm afraid that I lead a very quiet life,' Lorna said dryly. 'You've been around the profession long enough to know that if a model gets to the top—and wants to stay there—too many late nights are the kiss of death!'

'I can understand that, but life would be very dreary and boring if it was a matter of all work and no play. I can't believe that you sit alone in your apartment every evening, for instance! Or do you, perhaps—er—live with someone . . .?' He raised a quizzical eyebrow.

Lorna was furiously annoyed to feel her cheeks flushing beneath the cool, penetrating stare from his brilliant blue eyes. 'The only person I live with is my sister,' she retorted icily. 'Not that it's any of your damn business!'

'My dear girl—of course it's my business!' he grinned. 'I don't particularly fancy the idea of an agressive boyfriend thumping me on the nose, just because I took you out to lunch! Besides,' he added with a grin, 'it seems a good idea to sort out the ground rules right at the beginning of our—er—relationship, don't you think?'

'What relationship . . .?' She gave a snort of derision. 'Never mind the ground rules, I don't even know what game you think you're playing!'

Alex laughed softly. 'What I have in mind is a very—er—loving relationship.'

She found herself rendered speechless for a few moments—almost winded by the sheer audacity of his words—before she at last managed to say with vehemence, 'You must be out of your mind! I thought I'd made it very clear, a few minutes ago, that I'm simply not interested. N.O. means *no!*'

'I never could spell,' Alex murmured as he calmly ordered the waiter to refill her glass, before changing the subject to enquire what she hoped to do, if and when her modelling career came to an end.

Lorna sighed, realising that it had been stupid of her to have responded so sharply to the teasing words of Alex, who was continuing to regard her with such a maddeningly warm and engaging smile. He was just the type of man who automatically flirted with every woman he met—between the ages of nine and ninety—and obviously nothing he said meant a damn thing!

'I haven't any real plans,' she began, and then to her astonishment found that she was telling him all about her interview with Mercy that morning.

'Since Mercy Bird is well known for having a mind like a steel trap, I should think she knows what she's talking about, don't you?' Alex mused. 'In fact,' he smiled and raised his glass, 'you'll probably make your fortune!'

Lorna suddenly realised that maybe Mercy wouldn't like her talking about the project quite so soon. 'It is still only an idea, so I'd be grateful if you didn't mention it to anyone just yet.'

'No one will hear about it from me,' he promised. 'In any case, you seem to be adept at keeping a low newspaper profile. Although I seem to recall ... Weren't you involved some years ago with the racing driver, Carlo Romani?'

'Yes, I was "involved" as you put it,' she said shortly, putting down her fork and shaking her head at any suggestion of dessert. 'Just coffee, please.'

'Didn't the poor chap die in some ghastly accident during a race?'

'Yes.'

'Were you still—er—living with him at the time?'

'If you're asking whether I saw him die: the answer is—yes, I did.'

Alex looked at her blank, frozen expression. 'I'm very sorry. I had no right to ask such a personal question,' he murmured gently. 'I ... I also owe you an apology for—er—last night. My behaviour really was quite appalling, I ...' he shrugged unhappily.

'You mean that you don't normally make a habit of being rude, and kissing strange women only five minutes after you've met them?' Lorna snapped, still feeling raw at being reminded of the terrible way Carlo had died.

He pushed a hand roughly through his thick, dark hair. 'For God's sake! No, of course I don't!'

'Wow! You mean I was just being treated to a free demonstration? Gee—that was real generous of you, Lord Kendall ... *ouch!*'

Startled, Lorna looked down at the large tanned hand grasping her wrist like a steel band, and then raised her head to meet his eyes which had become clouded and stormy with anger. She shivered, suddenly remembering the glimpse she'd had last night of the menacing force which lay below his charming surface, before taking a deep breath and icily telling him to let go her hand.

'Certainly. However, the next time someone genuinely tries to say that they're sorry,' he purred dangerously, 'try and remember your manners, hmm?'

He really was incredible! Lorna simmered with rage as she massaged her sore wrist. Not only had he behaved disgracefully last night, but now he was having the damned cheek to try and make *her* feel guilty—she had had it! Putting down her serviette, she rose to her feet. 'Thank you for lunch,' she said coldly, before turning and walking quickly towards the door.

'You spoilt your—er—grand exit by forgetting your coat!' She turned to meet Alex's mocking grin as he stood beside her on the sidewalk and waved down a cab. 'You mustn't catch cold,' he murmured, draping the coat over her shoulders, swiftly lowering his head to brush his mouth over her lips before opening the door and allowing her to get into the vehicle.

Lorna sat back in the seat, grinding her teeth with rage and stonily ignoring Alex's mocking smile as the cab drove away. He was, without doubt, the most annoying man she had ever met, and she never— *positively never*— ever wanted to see him again!

CHAPTER FOUR

SIGHING deeply, Lorna put down her pen and stared blankly out through the window. Normally she loved to sit at her desk, the living room only lit by the soft lamps as she gazed at the inky darkness of the night, illuminated only by the neon glow and twinkling lights of Manhattan. Tonight, however, she simply didn't seem to be able to concentrate on either the view or on the papers before her. Getting up to go over and pull the curtains, she gave another sigh before returning to try and make some sense of the figures she had been studying.

Having drawn up a 'for' and 'against' list, she had still not found a solution as to whether or not she should become Mercy's partner in the new venture. Her instinctive reaction that it would be fun, was now being tempered by the realisation of just what a gamble she might be taking. If it meant that she was the only person involved, the decision would be simple. However, no matter how she did her sums, the amount of money required for her share of the partnership would leave her dangerously short—especially if money was required in the near future. She'd gone into the modelling business with the sole aim of supporting herself and Beth. Surely it would be foolish to now fall at the last fence, just because of a bad investment? On the other hand, as Alex had so rightly said at lunch, Mercy did indeed have a mind like a steel trap, and if she thought it was likely to be a successful venture . . .?

At the thought of Alex Kendall, Lorna gritted her teeth and tried not to look at the large pot of flowering white gardenias set on a small table by the couch. She had been delighted to receive the plant which had arrived by special messenger that morning. But by the time she had read the enclosed note, she was no longer smiling and had unceremoniously dumped it in the kitchen.

'You can't leave such beautiful, delicate flowers in there,' Beth had protested when she had arrived back home a few hours ago. 'Who sent them?'

'That awful man, Alex Kendall. If you like them so much—you're welcome to them!' Lorna snapped.

'Well, I don't like the man either, but you must admit it's a lovely gift. I wonder why he sent it?'

'After the row I had with him at lunch yesterday—so do I!'

Beth looked at her sister in surprise. 'You never told me that you'd met Alex again. Has he changed his mind about Harry and me getting married?' she asked eagerly.

Lorna could feel her face flushing with embarrassment. She wasn't entirely sure just why she hadn't said anything to Beth about the disastrous meeting with Alex, and how could she now possibly even begin to explain why the subject of her sister's marriage hadn't arisen?

'Well?' Beth demanded impatiently. 'What did he say?'

'I —well, the truth of the matter is . . .' Lorna took a deep breath. 'I'm terribly sorry, darling, but we didn't somehow get around to discussing you and Harry. I—I honestly don't know why, really I don't.' She shrugged helplessly, knowing how much her confession would be hurting Beth.

'But—but you must have said something . . .?' The wounded grey eyes looked at her reproachfully.

'All we did was to have an argument. He and I—well, we just seem to rub each other up the wrong way whenever we meet,' she smiled contritely at her sister.

'To be honest, I think if I had said anything, it would only have made matters far worse for you.'

'I expect you're right,' Beth muttered dully, her shoulders slumping as she trailed away to her room.

Lorna had been left feeling ashamed and guiltily aware that, for almost the first time in her life, she had failed her sister.

Gazing down now at the papers covered with figures on her desk, she realised that she wasn't going to make any constructive decisions, not while her mind was so full of other matters. Besides, it was time she went and had a bath, since Jay Holden would be calling to take her out in just over an hour's time. She'd tried to ring his office earlier, to say that she wasn't feeling very well—or some such excuse— but his minions had been unable to trace him. So, it looked as if she was stuck with her dinner engagement, although she firmly intended to make it the last date she had with the millionaire. She had quite enough to think about at the moment, without having to cope with his determined courtship.

As she lay soaking in the hot, oily water, Lorna tried to think how she was going to make it plain to Jay that she wasn't interested in either him, his millions or his frantic lifestyle. None of which would be important if she really loved the man, but since her only feeling for Jay was one of casual friendship, the sooner she made it clear she wasn't interested the better.

The trouble was, she thought, stepping out of the bath and wrapping herself in a warm towel, of all the hundreds of attractive men she had met in the last three years since Carlo's death, not one of them had caused her to lose even a night's sleep. Walking through into her bedroom, she recalled how shocked and angry her father had been when she had announced that she was leaving America, and going to live with Carlo Romani.

'My God, Lorna, you can't be so foolish!' he had

thundered. 'You've just won the "Most Promising Newcomer on Broadway" award, besides having the option to go to England with the production; and now you're telling me that you are going to leave the cast and fly off to Rome with that crazy Italian racing driver? You must be out of your mind!'

She had tried to explain how much she loved Carlo, but when her father either wouldn't or couldn't understand, she had known that she had no alternative but to listen to her heart. She had never regretted her decision, and in the two precious years that she and Carlo had spent together, she had been supremely happy. They had meant to get married straight away, but the hectic life of the motor racing circuit was such that they kept putting off the day. Somehow, it hadn't seemed important when they were so much in love—and with all their life before them, what did a few months' delay matter?

When Carlo had been so tragically killed, the news of the multiple crash involving two other deaths had flashed around the world. It was then that she realised how much her father really loved her. Despite his angry words and the resulting two years' silence, Lawrence had arrived the very next day to see to all the formalities and to lead her shattered, trembling figure to the specially chartered aircraft he had waiting to fly them back to New York. He had been wonderfully warm and tender, especially during the following weeks as Lorna struggled to comprehend the terrible finality of Carlo's death. It was a double tragedy that the time she and her father had spent getting to know each other again, should have proved to be all too short; ending three months later in his own death in a car accident.

I don't know why I'm feeling so gloomy and introspective tonight, Lorna thought, slipping into a long, black woollen cashmere dress and hunting through the closet for her favourite pair of gold evening slippers.

Carlo had been dead for three years now, and the passage of time had eased most of her grief at his loss. Nothing could diminish the love they had experienced, but during the last few, hectic years when she had been working so hard to support herself and her sister, the pain of his loss had gradually lessened until now she was left with warm, happy memories of their time together. Only when a reference was made to his death, as Alex had done at lunch yesterday, was she forcefully and painfully reminded of the terrible sight of Carlo's body in flames . . .

Alex! That damned man was beginning to get under her skin! Sending her those gardenias might seem a friendly gesture, but she suspected that he had done so in the deliberate knowledge that a plant would be far more difficult to throw away than mere flowers. And after she had read the enclosed note, she was certain! 'To the fairest of the fair,' the swine had written. 'I send these flowers as *a constant reminder* of my love for you—which is as pure as these white petals! Alex.'

Ha-ha! Very funny! Lorna scowled, wincing in pain as her fingers angrily jabbed a hairpin into her scalp. She must stop letting that man wind her up, she told herself sternly. He was only going to keep on teasing her while he was sure of getting a reaction. She certainly wasn't going to see him again, of course, but if the worst should happen, she must make sure that she remained cool, calm and collected—whatever the provocation!

'Golly! You look sexy tonight.' Beth seemed to have recovered from her disappointment, smiling up from the piano as Lorna put her head around the door of the soundproofed music room. 'I thought you didn't really care for Jay Holden? Still, if he sees you in that dress . . .' She played a few bars of the Mendelssohn Wedding March.

'Ha! Very amusing!' Lorna grinned, before looking down apprehensively. 'Is the neckline really too low? I certainly don't want to give Jay any ideas he hasn't got already, but it's so cold outside and this is the warmest evening dress I could find.'

Beth looked at the soft woollen garment, clinging to every curve of her sister's slim figure. The deep plunging V of the neckline was edged in a thin band of black sequins, with further sequins around the cuffs of the long sleeves. There was no doubt about it, Lorna looked ravishing, especially with her hair in that heavy coil at the back of her head, the large gold and jet stud earrings emphasising her long slender neck.

'No, I was just teasing. There's nothing to worry about, you look great!'

'Help! There's the door bell—I must fly. Don't practice too hard, and remember the steaks are in the ice-box, OK?'

Later that evening Lorna sat toying with a glass of champagne, wishing her sister had been more ruthlessly honest. Jay had taken one dazed look at her as she took off her coat in the restaurant, and had been heavily gallant all evening. She knew he was working himself up to propose to her, and she was finding it an exhausting task trying to head him off. Even now, here in the '21' Club, Jay was unstoppable as he related one business coup after another. Each story seemed designed to illustrate what a formidable opponent he was, although Lorna found herself feeling more and more sorry for those he had crushed underfoot.

A waiter came up to their table. 'Excuse me, Mr Holden, but there is a telephone call for you. Do you wish to take it here at the table?'

'No, tell 'em I'm busy, OK?' Jay barked, pushing some money into the waiter's hand before turning back to Lorna. 'Now, Lorna, where was I? Oh, yes. There were these Arab boys who thought they were going to take old Jay to the cleaners, but I sure fixed them! What I did was . . .'

Lorna turned away to try and politely hide a yawn, suddenly stiffening with shock as her eyes met those of Alex, who was sitting with a large party further along the wall to her left. Even from where she sat, she could see the sardonic glitter in his blue eyes as he raised his glass in mocking salute. Schooling her face into immobility, she forced herself to stare disdainfully right through him, as if she had never seen him before in her life, before turning back to smile brilliantly at Jay.

'So you like hearing about my business deals, huh?' he beamed at her, his chest swelling with satisfaction and pride.

'I just love it,' she breathed ecstatically. 'Do tell me some more!'

This has got to be the Oscar-winning performance of all time, she told herself as she gazed lovingly into Jay's eyes. Alex was clearly convinced that she had deliberately gone to the Museum, yesterday, just to meet him. Well, this was a perfect opportunity to show him that far from being struck by his manifold charms, she had plenty of other interests to occupy her time— including the richest man in New York! She knew it was fairly rotten of her to use Jay in this way, but the urge to show Alex that she simply wasn't interested, was proving irresistible.

Lorna's rapt attention to Jay's monologue was interrupted by the appearance at their table of a young man dressed in a formal business suit. 'I'm very sorry to disturb you, Mr Holden, but we've got a slight problem. The bourse in Paris is about to close, and all of a sudden the bottom is dropping out of Lachaise stock. Knowing how large our holding is ...' he paused, looking at his employer for instructions.

Jay glanced at the time and then, rather as a snake might slough a skin, so he cast aside the veneer of a pleasant if somewhat boring escort revealing the formidable, ruthless force with which he had carved his way through the business jungle.

'It's another hour before the Stock Exchange in London closes for business. I'll get to a phone and see if I can off-load some of the stock, while you'd better find out what's happening—even if it takes you all night,' he said to his young assistant, his voice heavy with menace. 'I'm sorry, honey,' he murmured, turning to pat Lorna's hand. 'I'll just be gone a few minutes.'

'There's no problem, I can easily get myself home . . .'

'Absolutely not,' Jay said firmly as he rose to his feet. 'I've got something I particularly want to talk to you about. So you just stay here, and I'll be right back, OK?'

Sitting back in her seat, Lorna tried to resist the temptation to sneak a look at the table to her left—and failed. Alex and his friends seemed to be enjoying themselves, if the noise and merriment were anything to go by. He had his arm draped around the shoulders of a beautiful girl with startling red hair, who was looking up at him in clear adoration. Bully for him! It looked as if he was set for a good evening, anyway.

The room suddenly seemed hot and claustrophobic, and she turned her attention to some of the other people present, trying to amuse herself with celebrity spotting; although she quickly noticed that her own presence was attracting some attention. Her face was so well known, that she ought to have got used to it by now, but she still felt awkward sometimes, especially as now when she was conspicuously sitting alone. Glancing at her wristwatch, she saw that it was well over half an hour since Jay had left. She couldn't keep sitting here like a lemon—God knows when he would be back, and it would be just like Alex to come up and make some snide remark. Hesitating for a moment, Lorna made up her mind and rose from her seat, threading her way through the tables towards the stairs.

'You are leaving us so soon, Miss Grant?'

'Yes, I'm sorry, Luigi, but I have to go,' she smiled at the waiter. 'When he returns, please would you tell Mr Holden that he can reach me at home tomorrow?'

She found that she had to wait for some time to claim her coat, the woman before her creating a fuss and claiming that something was missing from a pocket. Shrugging herself into the grey fox fur, she was grateful for its warmth as she stood waiting outside on the sidewalk while the doorman went to call a cab.

'You wanna go somewhere, lady?'

'Yes, I . . .' she looked up, her eyes widening as she viewed the bright red monstrosity which had drawn up before her shivering figure. It—it looked like something which had been made in the nineteen thirties, with four, huge chrome metal coils issuing from the automobile's engine and curving away under the chassis. Her incredulous gaze flowed over the vehicle, and it was only then that she noticed the driver.

'Hurry up and jump in, love.' Alex grinned. 'It's bloody freezing out here!'

Totally confused, she noticed that it was a two-seater, the soft white top of the convertible being folded down over the boot. 'What—what on earth do you think you're driving, for heaven's sakes!' she gasped, before finding herself giggling helplessly at the sight of Alex wearing a Sherlock Holmes type of hat, with flaps hanging down over his ears.

'Lovely, isn't she?' he enthused. 'A modern replica of the Duesenberg "J"—Al Capone would have adored one of these!'

'You—you're crazy! You don't seriously expect me to drive around like a gangster's moll in that contraption? Forget it!' Lorna told him as she tried to stop laughing.

'*Chicken!*' he taunted.

'I'm no chicken,' she retorted. 'I just don't see why I should freeze to death.'

'How about if I make the supreme sacrifice, and offer to lend you my hat . . .?'

'My God—no thanks!' Lorna glanced up and down the deserted street, searching for a glimpse of the doorman who was supposed to be finding her a plain, ordinary, everyday New York cab. 'Oh . . . all right,' she shrugged helplessly. 'But I hope to heaven that you're insured to drive this—this extraordinary vehicle?'

'To the hilt,' he assured her, grinning as she hitched up her skirt and got in beside him. 'Now, if Madam would tell me where she wishes to go, I will endeavour to drive Madam there with all despatch.'

'Madam says: "Home, James! And don't spare the horses!"' she laughed, before being jerked hard back against her seat as Alex engaged the powerful Ford V8 engine, and they roared off down the street.

Not bothering to attempt to make any conversation, Lorna huddled down in her seat, clutching her fur coat tightly about her ears. Although, in fact, the seats were set so low that the high windshield offered considerable protection against the wind.

'I hope you've enjoyed your trip,' Alex said as he brought what she thought of as 'the red monster' to a halt outside her apartment block.

'I can hardly bring myself to admit it—but yes, I did!' she grinned. 'Now, how in the hell do I get out of this thing?'

'No problem,' he murmured, stepping out and coming around to open her door. 'I'd better see you safely upstairs to your apartment.'

'There's no need, I'll be quite all right. Thank you for the drive home,' she said firmly. Giving him a cool, dismissive nod, she walked quickly through the door and across the hall to the elevator; only to stand clicking her teeth with annoyance when she found the doors didn't open immediately.

'Don't you think the chauffeur ought to be rewarded with a drink?'

Lorna almost jumped out of her skin at the dark, drawling tones of the voice behind her shoulder. She hadn't heard his approach—the man must walk as silently as a cat. No, not a cat, she decided, glancing swiftly up through her lashes at the amused grin on his tanned face. In fact, a sleek, lithe panther—handsome but notoriously dangerous animals—would. be nearer the mark.

'You shouldn't drink and drive,' she said, staring fixedly at the elevator and willing it to arrive so that she could escape.

'OK, I'm not too proud to ask for a cup of hot coffee. Surely you can't begrudge me that? It's very cold outside,' he added plaintively as the elevator doors flew open.

'Well, if you will drive around in such a ridiculous automobile, what do you expect?'

'You're a hard-hearted woman, Lorna Grant!' he laughed. 'I thought you'd enjoyed your drive?'

'Yes, well, so I did, and I've already said that I'm grateful,' she muttered, trying to tear her eyes away from the warm curve of his smiling mouth. 'Anyway, what about your friends?'

'What about them?'

'They—they were still at the club when I left, and . . .' she shrugged.

'I decided to drive you home, because I don't like to see a poor girl deserted by her date . . .'

'I wasn't deserted!' she protested, flushing with anger.

'. . . and if I wanted to be with them, I wouldn't be here, would I? Especially since it cost me a fortune to bribe the doorman *not* to find you a cab!' he continued, one eyebrow lifted in sardonic amusement.

Really! He was impossible! How dare he insinuate that she had been stood up by Jay? Not to mention practically shanghaiing her from outside the '21' Club? Lorna opened her mouth to give him a piece of her mind, and then shut it again quickly as she remembered her own advice to herself, earlier in the evening: advice that was easier to say than to carry out, she acknowledged as she fumed with a frustrated longing to slap his smiling face. She had never known anyone who exuded such arrogant, confident masculinity, who was capable of making her so shockingly aware of his powerful sexuality. She had met many men who were far more good looking, but none whose sheer physical impact could provoke her with such consummate ease, causing her to feel light-headed and breathless, just by smiling down at her as he was now . . .

'Come on, give me your key.'

'What . . .?' she looked up, startled to find that they had arrived outside her front door. How on earth had they got here? She had absolutely no recollection of . . . Her cheeks flushed as she hunted in her evening purse. You've got to pull yourself together! All the man wants is a cup of coffee, for heaven's sake, she lectured herself sternly as he took the keys from her nervous fingers.

'My—my sister will be asleep, so I don't really think that . . .' She found that she was being gently but firmly led into the dimly lit hall of her apartment.

'Then we'll have to make sure that we're quiet, won't we?' The vivid blue eyes were glinting wickedly as they watched the confused alarm which swept over her face.

'Well, I . . .'

'It's all right, Lorna. I've registered the message that you've got a built-in chaperon,' he drawled with sardonic amusement. 'So, why don't you relax, hmm?'

He's right, she thought as he helped her off with her coat. Really, what had got into her? She wasn't a young girl of sixteen out on her first date. She'd been around town for a long time now and certainly ought to be able to handle any situation. This man had merely brought her home, and it was an entirely reasonable request that she should give him a drink before he left.

Leading the way into the living room, she switched on the lamps whose soft glow gave the room a warm, intimate atmosphere she felt she could do without. The feeling was intensified as she watched him shrug off his coat to reveal a superbly cut dinner suit, emphasising his broad shoulders and the long length of his legs. He—he really is devastatingly attractive, she thought suddenly, her eyes drawn to the dark hair curling over the stiff collar of his evening shirt, the white silk contrasting so strongly against his tanned face.

'Despite your warning on the dangers of the demon drink, I think I'd prefer a brandy, please,' Alex drawled.

Lorna walked over to the small bar in the corner of the room on unsteady legs. Despite his innocuous words, the warm caressing tone in his voice had left her feeling breathless, while her pulse seemed to be racing almost out of control. With shaking hands she tried to pour the correct measure into the glasses.

'Hey—whoa . . .!' he laughed softly, coming over to take the bottle of brandy from her trembling fingers.

Her nerves jangling like alarm bells at his warm touch, she stared stupidly down at the glass surface of the bar, completely unable to move away from the tall figure standing so close beside her. Almost as if it were happening to someone else, she found herself being turned towards him, while a hand beneath her chin was gently, but firmly, tilting her face upwards. Time seemed to hang suspended, holding her imprisoned like a fly in amber as she stared mesmerised up into his eyes; the darkening, unmistakable gleam from beneath his lids causing her body to shake and quiver. It was only when she felt his strong arms closing about her figure, that the mists began to clear away and she found herself slowly returning to normality. Her eyes widened, the gold flecks in their green depths flashing with alarm.

'Shush ... relax, you lovely girl,' he murmured, feeling her body tense against him as his lowered his head to softly brush his lips across her mouth.

'No ...!' she gasped, trying to ignore the wild beating of her heart and an insidious, rising tide of sensual excitement which flowed like quicksilver through every part of her body. Helplessly, Lorna felt her lips part beneath the deepening force of his kiss, recognising a desire she hadn't felt for years awakening inside her. Sliding her arms up around his neck, she responded blindly and with an increasing urgency to the hard, male body pressed so firmly against her softly yielding breasts and thighs.

Alex's lips moved to trail down to the wildly beating pulse at the base of her throat, before he slowly raised his head, his glittering blue eyes intently studying her face.

As she tried to clear her dazed vision, she realised that she was still held fast in his arms, shivering with reaction to the storm of passion which his kiss had awoken within her.

'Lorna ...' His voice was a husky whisper as his hands moved to withdraw the pins from her hair. 'So beautiful ...' he breathed, burying his face in the fragrant, heavy gold mass as it fell freely about her shoulders, before his mouth claimed her lips again.

Just for a moment she closed her eyes, allowing her senses free rein as she inhaled the musky scent of his cologne, the aching need to submit to the melting heat of his fingers, sliding down through her hair to caress the soft curves of her body. Then the sensual mastery and the shattering possession of his kiss hardened, demanding a response that sent shockwaves spiralling through her brain. It forced reality upon her with such startling clarity that she managed to find the strength to push him violently away. Shuddering under the tension of her own emotions, she stumbled away to collapse on to a couch.

'What is it? What's wrong?' Alex demanded, striding over to sit down beside her and clasping her trembling hands.

'I . . . I'm sorry . . . I should never . . .' Her voice was husky with self-contempt as she tried to control the stupid, weak tears that clouded her vision. Lorna's cheeks burned with shame at having so easily succumbed to Alex's overpowering attraction. Not since Carlo's death had she ever . . . And with Alex—of all people!

'Come on, you lovely girl, there's no need for tears,' he said, reaching into a pocket and passing her a large handkerchief. 'I must say,' he gave a wry bark of laughter, 'I've known some women to cry at the end of a love affair—but not before it's even started!'

'I d-don't w-want to have an affair with you!' she stuttered, blowing her nose fiercely and trying to stop her hands from shaking.

'Oh yes, you do,' he replied, the calm certainty in his voice bringing a rising tide of anger to her aid.

Jumping to her feet, she tossed the long hair from her face as she glared at him with fury. 'One fine day, Lord Kendall, it's going to dawn on you that you *aren't* God's gift to women, and—and I hope you manage to survive the shock!'

'Bravo!' he smiled, rising to his feet and moving to stand looking down at her. 'Something tells me that this is where I should make a graceful exit—especially since you seem to be reverting to your normal, sweet self! However,' he paused, the cynical smile dying from his face as he gazed into her flashing green eyes, 'you really must learn to stop fighting both me and yourself, Lorna. We'll both be a lot happier if you do.' The soft words hung menacingly in the air between them, before he turned away to pick up his coat.

'Why, you insufferable—arrogant . . .' Lorna was too full of boiling rage to think of any more epithets, nearly exploding as he laughed and blew her a kiss on his way out of the room.

Not until she heard the front door close softly behind him did her rigid, trembling figure relax. She felt totally drained of all emotion as she forced her weary body into her bedroom, undressing and falling into bed where she fell immediately into an exhausted sleep.

Lorna had hardly surfaced the next morning, feeling sluggish and heavily lethargic, when Beth bounced into the room. 'Did you have a good time last night?' Luckily, her sister was busy drawing back the curtains, and didn't notice the hectic flush which she could feel sweeping over her face.

'It was all right,' she muttered in a non-committal voice, and was relieved to see that Beth was far more interested in discussing her own news.

'Guess what?' she smiled radiantly at Lorna. 'Harry phoned last night, just after you'd gone out. He said to forget anything Alex may have said; his cousin was only giving in to the combined nagging of his aunt and mother.' She danced across the room with excitement. 'Apparently Harry has put his foot down, and now his mother is very happy about us getting married—how about that!'

'How about that . . .' Lorna echoed, trying for her sister's sake to suppress her severe reservations. She somehow didn't feel that Harry's mother would really have given in so easily, not when she'd gone to all the trouble of sending Alex around to see Beth.

'What's more, Harry's mother is writing to formally invite us to stay with the family for Easter!' Beth hugged herself ecstatically. 'I can hardly believe that it's all going to come right, at last. You will come over with me, won't you, Lorna? Mrs Kendall's invitation includes you as well.'

'Honestly, darling, you know I'd come and support you if I could. However, I'm absolutely certain that I'm booked to film an ad, and I really can't get out of it. I do have two days free then, but that's simply not enough time to be of any help to you.'

'Oh Lord—I'll never be able to cope with all those strangers on my own!' Beth was suddenly cast down into the depths of despair.

'Yes, you will,' Lorna told her firmly. 'Harry obviously loves you enough to have put up quite a fight with his family, and that's what you must cling to.' She swung her feet out of bed. 'Now, I must get up. However, if I should find that I'm free, I promise that I'll come with you like a shot, OK?'

'Thanks, Lorna,' Beth gave her a hug. 'Maybe they'll change the date for filming the ad—they often do.'

'Don't count on it,' Lorna warned her before disappearing into the bathroom. Slowly brushing her teeth, she resolutely tried to close her mind to the events of the previous evening, and concentrate on her sister's news instead. She still hadn't asked Beth about her plans for her musical career, for instance, and that was something they must talk about very soon. Beth was sure to ask her advice, and she wished she knew what it ought to be.

If only *she* had someone to turn to, someone to give *her* some good advice—God knows she needed it! It was no good getting all het-up about last night, since obviously Alex had only been giving full rein to his normal, red-blooded self. It was her own weak submission to his kisses which was particularly disturbing and she now saw, only too clearly, that the whole situation had been her own stupid fault. She'd behaved like a silly little teenager in the club. If she'd bothered to stop and think about what she was doing, when she had so conspicuously ignored Alex, she would have realised that for his sort of man, her behaviour had been a challenge he couldn't ignore. He obviously hadn't been able to resist proving his overwhelming mastery of women—and she'd fallen into his hands like a ripe plum, hadn't she?

Lorna squirmed with embarrassment, trying not to look at her flushed face in the mirror as vivid images of last night filled her mind. You knew what he was like! You knew that he was just a collector of women's scalps—so how could you have been so damn stupid? she accused herself, bleakly aware that it was her treacherous body which had overruled all sense and caution. She had only ever made love with one man in her life, and although since his death many men had made it plain that they were interested in more than a platonic friendship, she had instinctively known that indulging in casual sex wasn't for her. And especially not with a professional seducer like Alex Kendall!

Two days later, towards the end of a particularly gruelling photographic session, Jay Holden finally contacted her. 'There's a call for Miss Grant,' one of the assistants called out across the studio.

'Take a message—can't you see we're busy?' Ashley Cooper growled, gesturing for the lighting to be altered so as to highlight the deep gold sheen of Lorna's hair.

'Mr Cooper, sir . . .' the young cameraman coughed nervously. 'It's . . . er . . . Mr Jay Holden for Miss Grant . . .'

Ashley gave a theatrical groan, but even he wasn't proof against the mention of the financier's name. 'OK,' he shrugged, 'we'll take a break—but only for five minutes, so don't get too lovey-dovey on the phone, darling. We still need to take some more shots.'

'Oh, for heaven's sake, Ashley! It's not that sort of thing at all,' Lorna muttered in annoyance as she went over to take the call

Putting down the receiver a minute or two later, she walked back with an abstracted air. Jay had been

unable to get away from his business affairs the night
they had dined together, and his phone call of regret
that he would be tied up, had been received at the '21'
Club only minutes after she left. But that, apparently,
wasn't why he had rung. The line had been very bad,
and she couldn't understand much of what he had said:
'The report in the paper expresses my sentiments
exactly!' had been the only phrase which had come over
with any clarity.

'How was Mr Money-bags?' Ashley teased.

'All right, I suppose,' she muttered. 'He was going on
about some report in the paper . . .'

'Yes, I saw it,' he laughed. 'You've been keeping
things very dark!'

'What on earth are you talking about?'

'Hey, Garry,' Ashley called out. 'Bring me a copy of
today's newspaper, will you? Yes, here we are,' he said,
folding the paper open at the page devoted to the gossip
column recording events in the lives of the rich and
famous. 'Shall I read it to you?' he asked Lorna as the
stylist came over to arrange her hair for the next shot.

She shrugged. 'Why not?'

'Let me see—yes, here we are. ". . . A little bird tells
me that also dining *à deux* were lovely, top model
Lorna Grant and the richest man in town, Jay Holden.
Going by the way they were gazing into each other's
eyes, readers of this paper can be confidently assured
that wedding bells are in the air. Watch this space for
their honeymoon news!" There you are, darling,'
Ashley laughed. 'Hot from the press!'

'It's all complete nonsense,' she said angrily. 'I'll sue
them blind!'

'Save your breath to cool your coffee,' Ashley
advised. 'Come on, we've got work to do.'

Lorna felt tired to death when she let herself into the
apartment later that afternoon. Not for the first time,
she wondered why she had ever taken up such an

exhausting profession. Rubbing the tired muscles in her neck, she went through into the kitchen to make herself a reviving cup of coffee. The kettle had just started to boil when she heard the phone ring, and with a sigh she lifted the receiver of the extension in the kitchen.

'You can't really be going to marry that appalling man, Jay Holden? He won't suit you at all, you know!' Alex's lazy, dark tones filled her ears.

'You've got a damned nerve! It's no business of yours who I decide to marry,' she said through gritted teeth. 'And—and how dare you speak about Jay like that!'

'Very easily!' Alex gave a mocking laugh. 'Come on, Lorna—you know very well that he's a ghastly bore, and that you'd have a thoroughly miserable life with him. My advice, for what it's worth . . .'

'Your advice isn't worth a dime!' she retorted furiously. 'So get off the line, *and get out of my life*!' she shouted, slamming down the receiver.

CHAPTER FIVE

LORNA was still seething with furious indignation when she answered the door bell an hour later.

'Hi—you were expecting me, I hope?' Her friend Candice stood hesitating in the doorway, peering doubtfully at Lorna's scowling face. 'I mean, you did ask me to come around for an early supper tonight, didn't you?'

'Oh God, yes, I'm sorry...' Lorna pushed a distracted hand through her hair. 'It's just been one hell of a day, if you know what I mean,' she smiled wearily as she led the way into the sitting room.

'Do I ever!' The Texan girl sank down into a chair, wincing as she eased off her shoes. 'I knew I should never have bought the damn things. I found them in that cute little shop in Bond Street when I was in London two days ago, and while I realised they were a bit tight, I simply couldn't resist the colour.' She regarded the emerald leather shoes with gloom, before turning to look at Lorna. 'What's up with you, kid?'

'Oh—just life, I suppose,' Lorna murmured evasively, moving over to the bar to mix them both a drink.

'Great! I sure need this,' Candice said, taking the glass and gazing at her friend with concern. 'You don't look in good shape, honey. Never you mind. You just tell your old pal, Candy, all about it, and you'll suddenly feel a whole lot better!'

'Idiot!' Lorna grinned and then shrugged her shoulders. 'It's nothing really, I suppose. I expect that I'm just being hyper-sensitive.'

She pulled out a cushion and sat cross-legged on the floor. So used to keeping her own counsel, and having always to appear strong and confident for Beth's sake, Lorna found that it took her some moments before she could bring herself to tell Candice about the sudden intrusion of Alex Kendall into both the lives of herself and her sister. Once she had started, it became easier, and soon she was pouring out the tangled tale of her encounters with the Englishman. 'And to cap it all,' she fumed, 'he had the brass nerve to phone me, just after I'd got in from work this afternoon. He'd read that silly report about Jay and myself in the gossip column—and gave it as his considered opinion that I really mustn't marry what he referred to as, "an appalling man"!'

'Wow! You've got a real tiger by the tail!' Candice laughed.

'I don't want the damned man, by the tail or anywhere else,' Lorna ground her teeth in frustration. 'Except to punch him on the nose—believe me, I'd *really* like that!'

'Look, honey,' Candice said quietly. 'You and me— well, we're not young girls any longer, right? So I'll lay it on the line for you, but I guess you've already worked it out for yourself, huh? You fell hard, like a ton of bricks for your Carlo, and the two of you had a good life together. But he's been dead for three years, honey, and you can't grieve for ever.'

'I'm not still grieving,' Lorna protested. 'I mean, of course I was completely shattered when he was killed, but that was three years ago. I—I sometimes feel guilty when I realise how ... how little I think about him these days ...'

'That's perfectly natural,' the other girl said firmly. 'You're young and healthy, and like you said, it's been three years. So what happens? Into your life walks Alex Kendall—that's what happens! I mean, not only is he a very gifted photographer, but he really is, without doubt, the sexiest thing on two legs that I've ever had the pleasure of meeting! I bumped into him at a party not long ago, and although we only talked for ten minutes, by the time our hostess pulled him away to talk to someone else, I was a shaking mass of jelly—even though I was having a really torrid affair with another guy at the time.'

'OK, so he's attractive . . .' Lorna shrugged.

'*Attractive?*' Candice threw back her head and roared with laughter. 'Who are you trying to kid? He's totally devastating! It sounds to me as if he's making a really big play for you, and you wouldn't be half-way human if you didn't want to respond.' She sipped her drink, looking at Lorna's bowed head, the heavy curtain of gold hair not quite hiding the hectic flush on her cheeks. 'Especially if you haven't been involved with anyone since Carlo . . .?'

'No, I . . .er . . . well, I've never really wanted to . . .' Lorna muttered, quickly getting up to pour them both another drink. 'I know it sounds crazy—I'm twenty-five years of age, for heaven's sake!—but I'm . . . well, I'm just not into picking up and discarding casual lovers, if you know what I mean. Not that I'm a prude or making any moral judgments on other people's behaviour,' she added hurriedly as she handed Candice her glass. 'It's . . . it's just . . .'

'Just not your "thing" . . .? Hell, honey, there's nothing wrong with that!' Candice smiled. 'What's more, only the other day I was reading a magazine article that said celibacy was now in fashion . . .! Not that I'd know much about the condition, I'm pleased to say!'

Lorna couldn't help grinning as Candice's laugh rang around the room. 'You can joke, Candy. But even if I'm prepared to admit that Alex is very attractive, I reckon that he's really only interested in trophy hunting—and I've got far too much pride to face the thought of *my* scalp hanging from his belt, thank you very much!' She sipped her drink. 'Do you remember

what happened to Marie Preston, who got involved
with that snake-charmer, Franco Martelli? He really
romanced the poor girl, who fell for him like a load of
bricks, before he gave her the old heave-ho and dumped
her a couple of months later. That was well over a year
ago. Nowadays, Marie's looking terrible, she doesn't
seem to care about her work any more and just spends
her time eating her heart out for the dreadful man—
who must have had hundreds of girls since he threw her
over! I may well be overdoing the self-preservation
bit—but even you must see why I don't want to get
involved with Alex!'

'Yeah, I guess so. While there's nothing so terribly
wrong about wanting to go to bed with him—it's
a perfectly normal reaction, believe me!—I can see that
for a serious girl like you, it would be *disasterville*! Boy,
that Alex Kendall . . . he sure gets around town!'

Feeling unaccountably depressed at having her instinctive judgment about Alex so forcefully echoed by
Candice, Lorna was saved from having to reply by the
ringing of the phone. Dreading to hear Alex's voice
again, she picked up the receiver gingerly, breathing a
sigh of relief to find the call was from Mercy.

'That was our dear agent, who wants to meet me for
lunch tomorrow,' she told Candice as she put down the
phone. 'I tell you what,' she continued quickly, before
her friend had a chance to say any more on the subject
of Alex, 'we've both had a hard day, so why don't we
take ourselves out to a movie? To show you what a
good friend I am, I'll even lend you a comfortable pair
of shoes!'

'You're on!' Candice grinned back. 'Just lead me to
them, honey.'

Sitting back and watching a blood-and-guts movie
which failed to hold her interest, Lorna realised that she
hadn't mentioned Mercy's Keep Fit venture to her
friend. Still, there had been quite enough discussion of

her private affairs for one night, she thought grimly as she resolutely tried to concentrate on the screen before her.

Beth was still up, studying a music score in the living room, when she returned to the apartment later that night. 'Hi, had a good day?' Lorna asked as she took off her coat.

'So-so,' Beth shrugged, putting down the manuscript. 'There have been some phone calls for you, I've put the names and numbers on your desk. Jay Holden rang twice!' she added with a grin.

'That's all I need!' Lorna grimaced. 'By the way, seeing you with that music reminds me ... What are you planning to do about your musical career if you and Harry decide to get married?'

There was a long pause as Beth looked down at her hands. 'I—I guess I've got to tell you,' she said at last in a small voice. 'I knew I'd have to, but like a rotten coward I've been putting it off.'

'For goodness sake—what's the problem?' Lorna asked with concern, coming over to sit down and put an arm around Beth's shoulders.

Beth took a deep breath. 'It's no good. It's taken me a long time to bring myself to face it, but I've now accepted the truth.'

'What truth?'

'I'd suspected the worst for some time, and when I asked my tutor to sock it to me—he did just that. I'm really sorry, Lorna, but he said that I'll never be a soloist—not a top flight one, anyway. Oh yes,' she tried to smile, 'I'd make a good accompanist, and I'll always be better than most piano players, but that's it.'

'What do they know?' Lorna retorted angrily.

'They do know and, more importantly, I know,' Beth said quietly. 'I just don't have what it takes, and that's the plain truth.' She looked sadly at her sister. 'The thing that hurts most of all, is that you've spent so much time and money on my tuition. I'm sorry, Lorna, I really am.'

'For heaven's sakes, that's not important. I just want you to be happy, darling,' she assured Beth.

'Well, in a funny way, now that I've faced up to it, somehow it isn't too bad. And Harry has been such a comfort. I'm not running away from failure and wanting to marry him on the rebound—nothing like that, I promise you. But, he's been so sympathetic and understanding about it all.'

'Oh Beth, I do wish you'd told me before now. I haven't been any help to you, have I?' Lorna felt crushed at the knowledge of how little she had done for her sister.

'You've done more for me than I can ever repay,' Beth said firmly. 'It's just one of those things, that's all. Having got that off my chest, at last, I feel so much better!' She hugged her sister with relief, and then yawned. 'Oh, Lord, it's time I was in bed. By the way,' she added as she left the room, 'I forgot to write down that Mercy's secretary phoned just before you came home. Apparently Mercy said to be sure and look glamorous for lunch tomorrow.'

Taking a cab downtown to the restaurant the next day, Lorna was still convinced that Beth must have been given a garbled message. What was so special about meeting Mercy for lunch? However, after staring discontentedly at everything in her closet, Lorna had decided on her old standby, the Yves Saint Laurent coat and matching dress. She had never regretted buying the plain, straight navy-blue woollen coat and silk dress two years ago, although it had seemed to cost a fortune at the time. The only concession she made to Mercy's request was to put up her hair and to wear a dashing, scarlet felt hat with navy-blue ostrich feathers curling around the brim. And if she doesn't think I look 'glamorous' enough—too bad! Lorna told herself as she made her way into the bar adjoining the restaurant.

Glancing around, she saw Mercy's unmistakable figure seated in a corner. She was gesticulating wildly as she talked to someone facing her, and Lorna had arrived at the table before she realised why that particular back view had seemed unaccountably familiar.

It was Alex Kendall! Lorna was so startled that she was struck dumb for a few moments, staring blindly up at his tall figure as he rose to greet her.

'Isn't it wonderful—this lovely man has decided to join us for lunch!' Mercy trilled. 'What will you have to drink, dear?'

'Oh—er—a dry martini, please . . .' she muttered, caught off balance by the shock of Alex's unexpected appearance.

'Alex tells me that you both know each other *very* well, isn't that a fantastic coincidence!' Mercy said with enthusiasm, before waving to a waiter and ordering Lorna's drink.

Lorna met the gleam in Alex's mocking eyes with an increasing sense of extreme irritation. She definitely didn't care for Mercy's inference that she was, or had been, one of his girlfriends. What was more, he might have mentioned that he was on friendly terms with her agent when she had told him about the Keep Fit project. She cudgelled her brains, trying in vain to recall exactly what she had said to him. What was he doing here, anyway?

Mercy soon enlightened her. 'I realised that you were worried about having to put up so much money for our little scheme . . .'

'Not so little!' Lorna said dryly, sitting down and trying to ignore Alex's presence.

'. . . Which is why,' Mercy continued, 'I know you'll be just thrilled to hear that dear Lord Kendall has agreed to join us. With his share, it will mean that you now only have to find a third of the sum I originally mentioned—how does that grab you?'

'By the throat!' Lorna retorted grimly. Exactly who propositioned who, I wonder . . .? she thought, turning to cast a jaundiced eye in his direction. It didn't need the sight of his mouth twitching in silent humour to have her worst fears realised. The swine had obviously thought that it sounded a good idea, and had approached Mercy behind her back. Lorna could feel herself growing tense and rigid with anger.

'You don't seem to be terrifically happy, dear,' Mercy said with a puzzled frown. 'Surely you can see that it would spread the load, moneywise, and it would also mean that our cash flow will be easier during the first few months,' she added, ticking the items off on her fingers. 'Really, you know, I do think that the addition of another partner can only be good.'

For whom? Lorna thought, burning with resentment at having been placed in such a cleft stick. Because, of course, Mercy was right—it was basically a very good investment. And if it had been anyone else, other than Alex, she would undoubtedly have welcomed the extra partner with relief.

'Just see if our table is ready, would you dear?' Mercy asked Alex, who smiled sardonically into Lorna's glowering face before rising to stroll leisurely across the room.

'OK, kiddo,' Mercy rasped urgently. 'We don't have much time. It's obvious that you don't like the idea of Alex Kendall coming into business with us—so what's wrong?'

'Everything!' Lorna groaned, realising that there was no way she could explain her complicated feelings about Alex—especially when she didn't entirely understand them herself.

'You'll have to be more specific than that—and hurry

up about it—he'll be back in a minute! Has the guy suddenly gone broke, or what?'

'No, I—I don't know anything about his business affairs . . .'

'Oh, for God's sake! Come on, Lorna, what's the problem with the man?'

Lorna shrugged unhappily. 'I—I just don't want to have anything to do with him.'

'*What?*' Mercy hissed incredulously. 'Are you trying to tell me, that simply because you don't particularly like the guy, you're prepared to blow up our whole project? God give me strength! He's not going to be involved in the day-to-day business, you know. We only want his money, for heaven's sake!'

'Well, I—I don't trust him,' Lorna muttered mulishly.

Mercy sighed. 'Look, he approached me and said he had some money to invest. Did I know of anything I could recommend? Well, I certainly did! He's perfect for our new venture dear, he really is—especially since he's a genuine aristocrat. His title will look great on the note-paper and our customers will just adore the thought of mixing with a real, live Lord!'

Lorna could feel her cheeks flushing with mortification. It was entirely her own fault that Alex was here today. If she hadn't told him about going into business with Mercy, none of this would have happened. Why, *oh why*, hadn't she kept her stupid mouth shut?

The older woman looked at Lorna's unhappy face. 'No one says you've got to like the guy. To put it crudely, let's just take his money and run—OK?'

Lorna sighed. There was nothing more she could say, was there? Mercy had intimated that her objections to Alex were childish—and she was right. In the cold light of day, Lorna's instinctive reaction to have absolutely nothing to do with him, didn't make sense. Neither did her first, overwhelming impression that he was joining

their new project for some reason other than purely
business. No one would be so stupid as to throw their
money away like that. She was going to have to,
somehow, swallow her pride and agree to accept their
new partner.

'OK, Mercy . . .' she sighed, 'we'll just have to see
how it goes, I suppose.'

'That's my girl!' Mercy sighed with relief as she saw
Alex returning. 'And don't worry,' she muttered. 'I'll
put him through the financial wringer at lunch and if
there are any problems, moneywise, I'll call the deal
off,' she promised.

'I haven't had a chance to tell you how very beautiful
you're looking today,' Alex whispered softly in her ear
as they followed Mercy's small, bustling figure into the
restaurant.

'Don't think that I don't know *just* how you wormed
your way into this deal!' she hissed, ignoring the
compliment as a waiter came forward to take her coat.
Sitting down, she busied herself in studying the menu
and then remained as silent as possible during the
ensuing meal. Not so, Mercy, however, who true to her
word, began to grill Alex about his business affairs.
Lorna was preoccupied with her own chaotic thoughts,
but she noticed that Alex seemed to be remarkably
unperturbed by Mercy's third degree tactics.

'Well, dear,' her agent said at last. 'Although we'll
have to get our lawyers to go over everything with a
fine tooth comb, I must say that this lovely man seems
to be in *great* financial shape!'

'I'm not sure that Lorna would necessarily agree,'
Alex drawled. 'She seems to have the extraordinary
notion that I and my family are on the verge of
bankruptcy!'

Lorna raised her head sharply, to meet the blue eyes
gleaming with amusement as she tried to control the
flush spreading over her pale cheeks. It was just like the

damned man to remember her wild accusations, issued when she had been so upset by his behaviour towards her sister, at their very first meeting in her apartment.

'Well, there's nothing wrong in being cautious, but I'm sure that Lorna's got the picture now,' Mercy said, smiling and patting his hand.

She certainly had! Lorna thought glumly. Far from being an impoverished nobleman, it appeared that Alex Kendall was extremely wealthy—unless the figures he had just been giving her agent were a load of garbage. However, Mercy was incredibly shrewd and could normally be relied on to see through any attempt at deception, although at the moment she seemed to be captivated by his handsome presence. Alex might be able to charm the birds off the trees, Lorna thought with fury, but he sure didn't fool her!

'. . . based here in New York at the moment?' A fragment of the older woman's conversation with Alex cut into Lorna's abstracted thoughts.

'Yes. My work takes me all over the world, of course,' Alex explained, 'but when I found myself doing more and more work in America, I bought a property so that I could have a permanent studio over here. However, as much as I enjoy life in New York,' he added with a smile, 'I must confess that I always look forward to returning to my real life—and real home—in England.'

'Well, dears,' Mercy said as a waiter served coffee. 'I guess that just about wraps it up for the moment. All we have to fix now are Lorna's photographs . . .'

'What photographs?' Lorna asked, looking up with a puzzled frown.

'We must have some good photos to launch our new project, of course,' Mercy said, looking at her in surprise. 'And, since dear Alex is now a partner, he has offered to take them for free—not bad, huh!' she smiled warmly at the Englishman.

'I'm sorry, that's just not possible,' Lorna said quickly and firmly. She might be over a barrel with their business venture, but there were plenty of pictures in her file which would do perfectly well—even if he was supposed to be one of the world's best photographers! 'I'm afraid that I'm fully booked up . . .'

'No, you're not, dear,' Mercy said, almost deliberately ignoring Lorna's words. 'The Garmonsway people rang up to cancel the session on Friday morning, and dear Alex has said he can fit you into his schedule. It all works out very neatly.'

Doesn't it just! Lorna fumed. Suddenly she'd had enough of the crowded restaurant, Mercy's euphoria at the addition of Alex Kendall as a partner and . . . and the sight of Alex, himself, smiling blandly into her angry green eyes. 'If you will excuse me, I'm afraid I have to go now,' she muttered, rising to her feet as an attentive waiter hurried forward with her coat.

'Here's my address,' Alex said standing up and holding out a card. 'I'll expect you at my studio at nine o'clock—so don't be late.'

'I am never late for my appointments!' Lorna snapped, angrily snatching the card. How dare he cast aspersions on her professional conduct! Turning to Mercy, she said through gritted teeth, 'As my agent, you might care to inform our new partner that I do not, *under any circumstances*, pose for salacious pin-ups— such as those normally taken of his many, oh-so-cute little girlfriends!'

The sight of the tight-lipped, dark fury spreading over Alex's face at her caustic words had been the only crumb of comfort in a quite terrible lunch, Lorna decided as she walked swiftly away. Sheltering beneath the canopy as a doorman called a cab, she thought that the rain pouring down from the dull, grey afternoon sky, exactly suited her mood of deep gloom and depression.

Lorna had originally planned to do some shopping after lunch, but on leaving the restaurant she felt so tired and depressed that she decided to go straight home. Entering her apartment, she realised with a sinking heart that once again she had failed her sister. Surely, at some point during lunch, she could have championed Beth's cause with Alex? She was positively neglecting her sister's affairs, she reproached herself sternly. She hadn't liked to ask too many questions, especially since the promised letter from Harry's mother had failed to arrive. Nevertheless, she ought to be a tower of strength at this difficult time in Beth's life, and it was only too clear—to herself, anyway—that she was being nothing of the sort.

It wasn't until a day later that she finally caught up with Beth, who had spent the previous evening with one of her classmates. Returning from filming a TV commercial, and wearily humping her tote bag into the apartment, Lorna heard her sister humming in the kitchen.

'Well, you certainly look bright and breezy,' she said, taking in the sparkling grey eyes and wide beaming smile. 'I know—don't tell me . . .! Harry has rung again?'

'Yes, *and* I got the letter from his mother! It's really nice, and says how much she is looking forward to seeing us—look!' She produced a much-folded piece of paper from her pocket.

'Hang on a moment,' Lorna smiled. 'Let me dump this bag and have a quick wash, and then you can tell me all.'

But Beth obviously couldn't wait, following her into her bedroom and sitting on the bed as Lorna put away her things. 'I've been so worried—well, you obviously knew I was. And I'm grateful that you didn't say anything. It would have made it all so much worse, somehow.'

Lorna was guiltily aware that her silence had been far more due to a preoccupation with her own affairs, rather than delicate sensibility towards those of Beth. Still, she would make up for it now, she promised herself, sitting down beside her sister and reading the letter. It didn't strike her as being particularly friendly, but was just a polite note asking the two sisters to come and stay during the Easter vacation.

'Isn't it a nice letter,' Beth said, clearly only able to view Harry and his family through rose-coloured spectacles.

'Yes, it is,' Lorna stoutly agreed. 'Is this their house?' she pointed to the engraved heading at the top of the letter. 'I must say that "Oakeley Park" sounds more like a stop on the subway, than a house.'

Beth giggled. 'I thought that too! But, in fact, it isn't really their house. It's all a bit complicated, but from what Harry said, I think it belongs to Alex, and they just sort of live there. Until Alex gets married, I guess.'

'I can't see him settling down in the near future!' Lorna said caustically, and then wished she hadn't. Any mention of Alex seemed to set her teeth on edge these days, and it wasn't fair of her to spoil Beth's happiness. He hadn't telephoned or tried to see her after the lunch with Mercy—and that was just fine by her!

'Harry says his mother is happy where she is, but his Aunt Caroline—that's Alex's mother—is very keen for Alex to get married. I sort of got the impression that the two sisters-in-law don't like each other very much! Anyway, Harry says that there is a perfectly good house in the grounds of the park for his mother, if and when Alex does marry someone.'

'What about you and Harry? Where will you live— not in the house with everyone else, I hope? I don't think that would be a good beginning for a marriage, somehow.' Lorna tried to put the warning as gently as she could. Having to move in to someone else's house, with a built-in mother-in-law, sounded like a quick recipe for disaster.

'Oh no,' Beth assured her, 'we won't be doing that.'

'That's a relief! So, what will you do?'

'Harry says that Alex is giving us an old farm house, and we can have all sorts of fun doing it up. Isn't it kind of him—Alex, I mean?'

It took Lorna some moments to recover from the shock of Beth's words. 'I had no idea—I mean . . .' She got up and went over to pull the curtains. 'I didn't know that Alex had changed his mind about you and Harry getting married. When did all this happen?'

'Didn't I tell you?' Beth looked over at the back of her sister's tall figure as she stood staring out of the window. 'I was sure I had, but I must have forgotten. Anyway, apparently Alex rang Harry some days ago, and said that I was a perfectly respectable girl . . .'

'Big of him!' Lorna muttered.

'. . . and as far as he was concerned, there was no reason why we couldn't get married. He even told his Aunt Sophie to stop meddling—how about that!'

Lorna tried to listen as Beth continued to extol Alex's virtues, but with every fibre of her being she wished that her sister would stop mentioning his name. She hadn't said anything about bringing Alex back to the apartment the other night, of course. It wasn't something she could possibly talk about, and she had done her best to expunge all thought of his lovemaking from her mind—with a singular lack of success. Having now decided, goodness knows why, to champion the young lovers' cause, Alex was obviously Beth's favourite man of the moment. And for the rest of the evening, Lorna had to suffer the constant reiteration of his name with as much fortitude as she could muster.

Lorna hestitated outside the front door of the building that housed Alex Kendall's studio, trying to summon up her courage for what she could only think of as a forthcoming confrontation. It was precisely five minutes to nine o'clock—Alex's remark: 'don't be late' still rankled—and if she could have thought of a good excuse for not being here, she'd have grabbed it eagerly with both hands.

She was surprised to find her knock answered, not by the sultry, luscious sort of girl she had expected, but by a middle-aged, efficient and charming receptionist, who led her up a flight of elegant stairs to the enormous studio. Alex and his two assistants were already busy at work and it was some moments before he noticed her presence. Clothed in a pair of tight, faded jeans, topped by a short-sleeved blue denim shirt which was unbuttoned far enough to display the dark curly hairs on his chest, there was no doubt that Alex was looking devastatingly attractive.

'Good morning, Miss Grant,' Alex drawled. 'And on time, too, I see!' he added, glancing pointedly down at the slim, gold Piaget watch on his bare wrist.

Lorna's lips tightened at the wry, sardonic note in his dark voice. She was trying to think of a suitably crushing reply, when the door behind her burst open to admit a noisy, chattering group of people.

'Hi, kid—nice to see you again.' John King, the hair stylist gave her a friendly pat on the shoulder, before turning to direct his two young, female assistants on exactly where to place the equipment they were carrying. 'And for God's sake be careful not to blow all the fuses today!' he growled at one of the girls as he walked over towards Alex.

'John's always *such* a sweetie, especially first thing in the morning!' The large, bulky figure of Danielle Moore, one of New York's foremost make-up artists, filled the doorway, smiling sympathetically at the young girl. 'Morning, Lorna. Did you have fun in Gay Paree?' she added with a grin, moving aside to allow the entry of two women submerged beneath bundles of clothing, and a stream of men carrying various pieces of gymnastic equipment.

'For heaven's sake! It's like a three-ring circus in here, and what on earth is that?' Lorna muttered, her eyes widening at the sight of a man at the tail end of the procession, valiantly trying to push a large, circular frame covered in white canvas, across the floor of the studio.

'"Circus" is probably the right word, darling, because that looks mighty like a trampoline, to me. I sure hope you're feeling fit, Lorna!' Danielle's heavy figure shook with laughter. 'Seems as though the glamorous Lord Kendall is going to make you jump through the hoops this morning!'

'That's all I need!' Lorna groaned, trailing reluctantly after Danielle towards the dressing room. She hadn't wanted to do this damn photographic session, she thought with grim apprehension, and it looked as if it was going to be every bit as dreadful as she had feared—if not far, far worse.

However, by the time she was dressing herself in her own clothes three hours later, Lorna had come to realise that Alex Kendall, the famous photographer, was a very different animal from the aristocratic Lord Kendall—or indeed Alex Kendall, the charming, dashing man about town. Whatever else he might be, there was absolutely no doubt of his complete and total professionalism. She would never have thought that she could be full of admiration for the man who had so disruptively invaded her life. But as she sat in front of the mirror, slowly combing her hair, Lorna had to admit that she had nothing but respect for his overwhelming flair and talent.

It had been the usual bedlam to start with, of course. Ignoring the noisy complaints of John, the hairdresser, as he harried his two assistants, and the bangs and thuds of the gymnastic equipment being moved around the room, Alex had quickly sorted through the leotards, tights and accessories ordered by Mercy.

'OK—that's it,' he said briskly, indicating a small pile in various shades of blue and green. 'You can take the rest back straight away.'

'But Mrs Bird quite clearly said that . . .'

'I don't give a damn what Mrs Bird may have said,' Alex retorted firmly. 'I am taking these photographs, and therefore *I* will decide what Miss Grant is to wear. That's the end of the discussion,' he added, calmly ignoring the woman's protests as he instructed Lorna to change into an emerald-green leotard: '. . . and be quick about it!'

Seething with rage, she nevertheless found herself reappearing back in the studio in record time, her anger slowly dying away as she realised that Alex hadn't just picked on her. She sat on a stool, watching as he ruthlessly—and impartially—proceeded to lay down the law to the crowd of people milling about the large room.

'Right. All you men from Raffles Gymnasium—get down the other end of the room. I'll let you know when I want some equipment moved, but until then I don't want to hear a sound from the lot of you!' He turned to the hairdresser. 'You can put away most of your equipment. I don't want any fancy business, John, just brush Lorna's hair so it lies in a stream down her back, OK? As for make-up, Danielle—keep it simple. Nothing heavy, but play up the eyes and the cheekbones.' Alex looked down at his watch. 'You've got ten minutes while I arrange the lighting. If you lot haven't finished by then—too bad!'

Danielle sighed dramatically. 'Why do I always forget what a damn dictator that man is?' she murmured, tilting Lorna's head back as she applied emerald green eye-shadow. 'I don't know why we put up with it.'

'Simple, darling,' John muttered, seizing a brush from an assistant. 'He's one of the best in the business, that's why! I mean, have you seen any of the photos that Leon Hardy's taken lately? God! I nearly died when I saw what he'd done to some of my creations—absolutely *el sicko* ...! Now, with Alex, one knows exactly what's what. He might be a damn perfectionist—but he sure delivers the goods. No hanging around for hours and hours, and a great set of photos at the end of the session. I'll happily work for him any day of the week.'

Five minutes into the session, Alex sighed and lowered his camera. 'This won't do at all,' he said, firmly grasping her hand and leading her rigidly tense, nervous figure over to a quiet corner of the room.

'I think we'd better get a few things straight,' he said quietly, his blue eyes boring into hers. 'First of all, my name is going to be on these photographs and I'm not prepared to produce anything less than my usual standard. Secondly, I want you to clear your mind of everything except the job in hand, right? I know that you wish you were a million miles away from here ...' He gave a dry bark of sardonic laughter. 'If it makes you feel any better, I got press-ganged into this job as well. Believe me, that agent of yours—dear Mrs Bird—would get blood from a stone!

'That's better,' he said as her lips stretched into a reluctant smile. 'Now, just to dot the "is" and cross the "ts", I can assure you that I never, *absolutely never*, mix business with pleasure—however great the temptation! So relax, hmm?'

As the session progressed, Lorna had been surprised to find that under his quiet, commanding and authoritative manner she was able to relax, managing to temporarily forget the emotional tensions that normally sparked between them. In fact, when he made her bounce up and down on the small trampoline—

something she had never done before—both they and the rest of the team became so convulsed with laughter, that it was some time before he managed to restore order.

'OK—that's it,' he announced at last, dismissing everyone except Lorna, whom he asked to stay on for some portrait photos.

'Mercy didn't say anything to me about wanting more portraits,' Lorna grumbled, perching herself on a stool in the empty studio.

'Didn't she?' Alex murmured, prowling back and forth as he intently studied the different angles of her face. 'Never mind, if she doesn't need them after all, you can always give them to your dear friend, Jay Holden!'

'He's not my dear friend!' she retorted, suddenly nervous at his close proximity. Now they were alone, she was vividly aware of his restless energy, the impact of his powerful, physical presence.

Alex gave her a cool smile, lowering his camera and moving lithely forward to turn her head a fraction to the right. 'Well, if you can't become ecstatic about your rich millionaire,' he mocked softly, 'maybe you should concentrate on thinking about Carlo?'

'Carlo . . .?' she queried huskily, barely comprehending his words as she gazed at the rapidly clicking camera, desperately trying to ignore his tall, dynamic figure, and the well-washed, faded jeans fitting so tightly over his taut hips and smooth muscled thighs. 'Why . . . why should I think about Carlo?'

He walked over to a tapedeck at the back of the room. 'I want some shots of you gazing lovingly into the lens,' he said as the slow, soothing strains of Rodrigo's *Concierto de Aranjuez* filled the air. 'You obviously don't want to talk about Jay Holden—not that I blame you!' he grinned. 'So, why don't you tell me about Carlo instead?'

'I—I don't see why you're interested . . .'

'I'm only interested in getting you to relax,' he said firmly. 'So, just calm down, and tell me all about it, hmm?'

Lorna shrugged helplessly. However, prompted by his murmurs of encouragement, she haltingly began to relate the story of her romance with Carlo. 'Then, after he died, I came back to New York with my father . . .' she concluded, her voice trailing away.

'It must have been very difficult to try and put your life together again,' Alex remarked quietly.

'Yes, yes it was,' she said, surprised and touched by his sympathetic understanding. 'Especially as my father was killed in an accident so soon afterwards. However, it did mean that I was so busy having to look after Beth and earn enough money for us to live on, that I didn't have any time to feel too sorry for myself—which I now see was probably a good thing.'

'You were obviously very much in love with Carlo. Do you still—er—still think about him a great deal?' Alex queried. Lorna glanced up quickly, but his voice and the blue eyes steadily regarding her over the top of the camera, conveyed nothing other than a mild, friendly interest.

'No, not really. I mean,' she strove to explain, 'it isn't that I've forgotten him—of course I haven't. But, somehow, as the years have gone by—well, it seems harder and harder to remember his face . . .'

'Which is quite natural,' he said firmly as he wound on the end of the film and ejected the cartridge. 'OK, I reckon I've got enough pictures to keep dear Mercy happy. You can go and change now, Lorna—you'll be pleased to hear your ordeal is over!'

Zipping up her tote bag, Lorna looked around the large, well-appointed dressing room to check that she hadn't forgotten anything. She and Alex had got on so well during the last part of the session, that she felt slightly ashamed. of both her initial apprehension and her rudeness at lunch, when Mercy had arranged the photographic session. Alex had obviously got the message that she wasn't interested in him, and she was even beginning to think that she might have been guilty of over-reacting to what had only been a casual flirtation on his part, when she opened the door and returned to the studio.

'Ah, there you are,' Alex said, standing beside a small table set with a bottle and two glasses. 'I think we ought to celebrate, don't you?'

'Celebrate? Celebrate, what?' She looked at him in puzzlement, her words punctuated by a loud bang as Alex removed the cork from a bottle of champagne.

'The fact that we're going to be so closely entwined— in business, I mean!' he drawled, his eyes sweeping over her tall, slim figure.

'You sneaked your way into *my* business, and I still don't know how you had the nerve! Why pick on our project, for heaven's sake?'

'I suppose because I thought it had—er—great potential!' He laughed as her green eyes flashed with annoyance. 'Darling, Lorna,' he murmured softly as he walked towards her. 'Don't you think that it's about time we kissed and made up, hmm?'

'Now, hold on just a minute,' she muttered, nervously backing away. 'I—I thought you said you didn't mix business and . . . er . . .'

'Pleasure . . .? Quite right!' he agreed, his eyes glinting with amusement. 'But we've completed our business, haven't we?

The sheer arrogance of the man! And what a stupid fool she'd been, thinking that he wasn't interested in her any more—she should have her head examined! Lorna could feel her temper rising as she attempted to make her feelings crystal clear. 'You can forget any "pleasure" you might have in mind! I must admit that

I—I've enjoyed working with you—but that's as far as it goes . . .' She felt her spine coming into contact with the wall behind her, her eyes widening with alarm as she quickly looked about for an avenue of escape from his tall, dominating figure. 'We have nothing to "make up" and I certainly don't want to kiss you . . . No! *Let me go . . .!*'

Gasping with outrage, there was little she could do as he leaned forward to pin her tightly to the wall, his hands firmly holding her head still beneath him. The mouth that possessed hers was warm and surprisingly gentle, softly teasing and slowly parting her trembling lips, evoking a response she seemed powerless to resist. She was only dimly aware of her emotions whirling and reeling out of control, her senses drugged and seduced by the devastating, erotic sensuality of his tongue as he savoured the moist inner softness of her mouth; her body treacherously and blindly responding to the increasing urgency of the hard frame crushing her against the wall.

'For someone who didn't want to kiss me—that's a remarkable performance!' Alex breathed thickly, lifting his head to look down at the passionate desire gleaming in her gold-flecked, green eyes.

'Please! Please . . . leave me alone!' she moaned, trying to gather her scattered wits.

'How can I, darling?' he murmured huskily, lowering his head to brush and tantalise her trembling lips. 'You must know how much I want you . . .!'

'The . . . the only thing I know, is that I . . . I'm an idiot to have come anywhere near you!' Lorna gasped angrily as she managed to wriggle out of his arms. 'They should lock you up and . . . and throw away the key!' she added, running over to grab her large tote bag and hugging it defensively to her chest. 'Now you get this—and get it straight—once and for all!' she hissed. 'I'm going to walk out of here, and if you take so much

as one step towards me, I'll start screaming "rape"—
and bring that nice respectable receptionist of yours
upstairs to see *just* how her randy employer treats his
clients!'

CHAPTER SIX

LORNA watched the stewardesses walking up and down the aeroplane, before turning to see if Beth wanted anything. Her sister seemed perfectly content, the earplugs she was wearing as she watched the movie making her deaf to Lorna's words. Grateful for anything that would take Beth's mind off her forthcoming meeting with Harry's family, Lorna leant back in her seat, wearily closing her eyes and trying to relax after one of the busiest and most stressful two weeks of her life.

Following the fateful lunch with Mercy and Alex, the business venture seemed to have taken off with a rush, gaining a momentum all of its own as the days passed. Their lawyers had drawn up the partnership details and it appeared that Alex Kendall really was as wealthy as Mercy had hoped. Almost incredibly, the first building she and Mercy looked at proved to be perfect, and they had made an immediate down-payment on the property. For all her harsh words and feelings towards Alex, Lorna was forced to acknowledge that it was due to his contacts that they had found just the right architect and designer to alter the interior. After a great deal of thought and argument between them, she and Mercy had decided to call their new, exclusive club by the simple name of 'The Place'. They had half-decided on 'The Body Beautiful', but as Mercy had pointed out in a midnight phone call: 'If I was a middle-aged man, I sure wouldn't want to go somewhere called that!'

If she had only been involved in helping to set up the new business, it wouldn't have been so bad. But having to try and keep up with her own hectic work schedule at the same time proved to be exhausting. Lorna had been just about to tell Mercy to try and lay off some of the jobs, when her agent had contacted her in great excitement. She had received a request from Adele Rootstein in London, the dynamic creator of the finest fibre-glass mannequins which were used to decorate the windows of all the top stores around the world.

'It's a great honour to be asked to model for her new collection of figures,' Mercy assured Lorna. 'The people she uses are usually film stars or well-known actresses— it's a regular hall of fame! So why don't I cancel that TV ad for the time being, and you can scoot off to London for a few weeks at Easter?'

'Well . . .' Lorna had hesitated, feeling so tired after a photographic session that she had difficulty in making up her mind.

'It will really do your career a lot of good, dear,' Mercy said, urging her to accept. It was primarily the thought that she would be available if Beth needed her help during her stay with Harry's family that finally persuaded Lorna to agree. Not that she was keen to visit Alex's home, of course, but since he was bound to be still in New York, maybe just staying a night at Oakeley Park to see Beth settled in, would be a good idea.

She had been convinced, when she had shouted those terse, rude words at Alex, that she would see no more of him. Quite certain, from the grim pallor of his face before he had spun on his heel and left the studio, that he would never want to set eyes on her again. 'You'd have thought he would have got the message,' she said indignantly to Candice, when they met for a drink one day after work. 'But not a bit of it! Everywhere I turn, I find that damn man staring at me—at the Opera with Jay the other night, on the street, in a restaurant— everywhere!'

'Well, you know how it is, honey,' Candice had

winked at her. 'It's the flowers that don't open, that attract the bees! Maybe if you just gave in, and said, "take me, I'm all yours", he'd leave you alone?'

'What great advice—thanks a million!' Lorna had groaned sarcastically.

'Hey! You mustn't let the man bug you like this,' her friend had laughed. 'Ignore him, and concentrate on Jay instead.'

Lorna sighed. 'He's another one who won't take "no" for an answer! I was as blunt as I could be the other night, but it didn't seem to make any difference. Luckily he's away in South America for a few weeks.'

Being kept so busy rushing from one job to another had certainly helped to keep her mind off Alex, and with only one day to go before she and Beth flew to England, it was early in the evening before she returned to her apartment. It had been her last session with Ashley Cooper, and she was feeling totally exhausted by the time she walked in through her front door. Longing for nothing so much as a long, long soak in the bath, she was thunderstruck to find Alex Kendall, wearing slacks and a cashmere sweater, sitting comfortably at his ease in one of her armchairs.

'What—what in the hell are you doing in here?' she gasped, almost not able to believe her eyes. 'How did you get in, for heaven's sake?'

'Your friend, Joe, the porter. He was very understanding when I explained my problem,' Alex drawled.

'Joe isn't going to remain my friend much longer, not if he does this sort of thing!' she snapped. 'And I'm now telling you to get up on your feet, and walk out of my apartment, OK?'

'Well, no. I'm afraid I can't just yet,' he said, smiling calmly at her. 'I had to see you, and breaking in here seemed the only way!'

'Oh God!' Lorna put her tote bag down on the rug

and slipped off her coat. 'I suppose it's too much to
expect you to understand, but I'm absolutely whacked.'
She ran her hands distractedly through her long hair.
'I've had a long, exhausting day, and all I want to do
now is to go and have a bath.'

'My dear girl, of course I understand,' he murmured.
'I know just how you feel. Go right ahead, and I'll
bring you in a strong drink—you look as if you could
do with one.'

'You'll do what . . .?' She gazed blankly back at him,
her senses responding to his warm smile and the
drawling, husky tone of his voice as her tired mind
struggled to comprehend what he was saying.

'I'm also, or so I've been told, very good at scrubbing
backs!'

'Do you mean to tell me . . .? You aren't seriously
intending . . .? *I don't believe it!*' Lorna stood aghast,
listening with horror as her yell of fury echoed around
the room. She must pull herself together, and quickly.
Closing her eyes for a moment to blot out the sight of
Alex's handsome, tanned face, she took a deep breath
and tried to calm down.

'OK, you've had your joke,' she said at last. 'I'm sure
you've got hundreds of girls just dying for your
company, *loverboy*, but I'm not one of them! So,
hello—and goodbye!'

'Are you really sure . . .?' he murmured, getting to his
feet and walking slowly towards her. 'Are you
absolutely certain that you don't want me here?'

'P-positive . . .' she stuttered, putting out a warning
hand as she backed nervously away. 'Quite . . . quite
certain!'

Alex continued to advance, his brilliant blue eyes
gleaming with a message that made her stomach lurch
wildly, and then tighten into a painful knot.

'My darling, adorable Lorna . . . what a delightful
liar you are!' he said softly, capturing her trembling

hand with ease and gently pulling her quivering body
into his arms.

'No . . .!' she groaned, trying to escape his embrace,
vainly trying to avoid the tanned face inexorably
descending towards her own. She was hardly aware of
the exact moment his lips touched hers, the soft, tender,
delicate movement igniting a sudden flash of excitement
that shot through her body. The intense heat of the
resulting explosion was so fierce, that she immediately
lost all sense of time and place. She knew only the
overwhelming need to respond to the powerfully
seductive, deepening kiss that tormented her senses and
sent the blood surging wildly through her veins.

Helplessly caught like a moth by the flames of her own
desire, she trembled violently as his fingers pulled down
the zip of her jump-suit, his hand moving over her firm
rounded breasts whose rosy tips hardened beneath his
touch. Moaning with pleasure, Lorna gave way at last to
the feelings she had hated to admit and had fought against
for so long. Her mind was too weary to control the
clamouring urge as mindlessly and involuntarily she
pressed her soft, yielding body closer to his.

Her action provoked a deep groan from Alex, and
the next moment she found herself swept up in his arms
as he carried her through into her bedroom, lowering
her gently on to the bed. Easing the jump-suit open to
display her breasts to his gaze, his mouth moving
erotically and languorously over her lips, before trailing
down her neck to the rapidly beating pulse in the
hollow of her throat.

'You're so lovely . . .!' Alex murmured thickly against
her skin. 'Only God knows how much I've wanted this!'
She shivered helplessly as she felt the warmth of his lips
on the taut fullness of her breasts, gasping as he
caressed one erect, swollen nipple and then the other—
his actions causing her to cry out with a pleasure so
intense that it was almost painful.

Alex raised his head a moment later, and looked at her through his lashes, his brilliant blue eyes now cloudy and sensual with arousal. 'You see,' he murmured hoarsely. 'I was right. You know you want me—just every bit as much as I want you, hmm?'

Despite the fever in her body, craving the ultimate fulfilment he was offering her, and aching with a deep, intense urgency which was almost overwhelming, Lorna shuddered as cold reality began slowly seeping back into her brain. Gazing up into his tanned face, darkly flushed with desire, she realised what it was that held her back from the edge of complete abandonment. It was the look of total certainty, the glint of triumph in his eyes . . .

'Yes . . .' she whispered, pushing him away and struggling to sit up. 'You . . . you are right. But wanting . . . wanting someone isn't enough—not for me, anyway . . . I'm . . . I'm sorry, Alex,' she added, feeling so tired and weary that she could hardly form the words. 'I'm sure—sure that having sex with you would be wonderful, but it . . . it wouldn't really mean anything, would it?'

He bent to kiss her bare shoulder. 'It would mean everything to me, darling,' he whispered huskily.

'For how long . . .?' Lorna sighed deeply. 'We're no longer kids, Alex, and we both know that there's all the world of difference between making love and just having sex . . .'

'For God's sake . . .!' Alex grated harshly. 'I can get sex anywhere—but I want to make love to you! You've captured my heart, and . . .'

'Heart? What heart . . .? You don't even possess such a thing!' she cried bitterly as she rolled off the bed, trying to do up her zip with hands that trembled uncontrollably. 'I sure got the message at lunch the other day! I'm not so dumb as you seem to think—and I know perfectly well that all you're interested in is a quick conquest, a nice little affair to pass the time, here in New York. Then it will be zip-zap . . . back to your real life and home in England! Well, *loverboy*,' her voice wobbled as she fought to control herself, 'I'm not prepared to be a temporary bit of home comfort, nor am I going to make love with someone who—who'd just regard me as another notch on his gun!'

'*How dare you!*' Alex snarled, leaping up and grasping her shoulders in a vice-like grip. 'That's a—a—disgusting and despicable thing to say . . . and totally untrue!' he ground out fiercely, his eyes flashing with anger, his tall figure shaking with rage. 'So, just who are you saving yourself for—that mighty lover, Jay Holden?' he taunted. 'Is it because he's richer than I am, hmm?'

'My God!' she gasped furiously. 'Now who's being despicable . . .!'

'Well, *darling*, if you're going to pick the ghastly Mr Holden—the very best of luck!' he drawled with cruel insolence. 'You'll certainly need it, both with him—and that old hag of a mother to whom he's *so* devoted!'

'Get out of here—*at once!*' she screamed, her body trembling with anger.

'Oh, don't worry—I'm going! But when you're miserable with your rich husband, don't forget to remember that I told you so!' Alex snarled, before stalking past her out of the room and slamming the front door loudly behind him.

Lorna's trembling legs collapsed as she threw herself across the bed in a raging storm of tears. Weeping all the more bitterly as she realised that although she had found the strength to send Alex away, she desperately longed to be in his arms once more . . .

'Hey—Lorna!' She looked up startled to see Beth smiling at her and pointing out of the aeroplane window. 'We're almost there,' her sister exclaimed. 'The stewardess has just told me that we'll be landing in England in twenty minutes. Isn't it exciting?'

Lorna smiled back as best she could, but felt only a nameless dread at the thought of having to become involved with Alex's family. Thank God his disturbing presence had been safely left behind them in New York.

The hour-long journey from Heathrow Airport into the centre of London was enlivened by Beth's excitement and nervousness over her first visit to England. 'I—I know it probably sounds weak and silly,' she muttered, 'but I do so want Harry's family to like me. I've been trying not to think about what Alex said when we first met him, but it's true, isn't it?'

'He said a lot of things, but only in the heat of the moment,' Lorna said. 'I shouldn't take any notice, and just wait until you meet them all.'

'It was when he said that if they don't accept me, that my life would be intolerable . . .' Beth muttered, not seeming to have heard Lorna's words. 'I do love Harry, but I don't suppose he will be able to be around all the time, will he? If they're horrid I—well, I guess I could get very lonely.'

'Now, come on. All this speculation is stupid, and you know it!' Lorna said briskly. 'I won't try and hide my feelings about Alex—I can't stand the damn man. But that doesn't mean that I'm not prepared to be fair. He seems to carry a lot of clout in the family, and he's gone to some trouble to make sure that you don't have a mother-in-law breathing down your neck; that offer of a farm house was really kind, wasn't it?'

'Yes, it was,' Beth admitted.

'Well, then—stop worrying! All you have to do is to be your own, sweet self, and there'll be no problem. Besides, Harry's got a twin brother and sister hasn't he?'

Beth nodded. 'Rupert and Augusta. They're about nineteen, I think.'

'"Augusta"?' Lorna raised an eyebrow. 'Ye Gods—what a name to call the poor girl! Still, that's one problem less for you to worry about.'

Her sister looked at her in confusion. 'I don't see . . .'

'Oh, Beth,' she sighed, torn between impatience and concern. 'There's no reason why a young girl shouldn't be kind and welcoming to her older brother's fiancée. If she loves Harry, she's going to try and like you, isn't she? And since you aren't exactly a nasty piece of work, I can't see that she's going to have any difficulty becoming almost as fond of you as Harry himself. OK?'

Beth grinned. 'I suppose you're right. Are we here?' she added, peering doubtfully out of the window at what seemed to be a large, red-brick mansion in a quiet Mayfair street. 'It doesn't exactly look like a hotel.'

'Well, I can assure you that the Connaught is a hotel, and one of the best in London—Father always used to stay here,' Lorna reassured her as the driver came around to open the door.

Waiting beside the reception desk as their booking was confirmed and the porters took their cases upstairs, Lorna decided not to tell Beth—especially after their conversation in the taxi—exactly why she had chosen to stay at this hotel. She had visited England many times in the course of her work, and had enjoyed staying in London. Nevertheless, she had few illusions about the majority of the English aristocracy's view of visiting Americans, whom they seemed to regard as strange creatures from another planet! That Alex Kendall had thought it necessary to assure his Aunt Sophie that Beth was 'a respectable girl', spoke volumes for their insularity—and she was damned if she was going to have some toffee-nosed old dowager looking down her nose at either Beth or herself! So, this visit—if only for her sister's sake—was going to be played straight from the rule book; there being no other hotel in London, other than possibly Claridge's, which carried the same weight of respectability as the Connaught.

'Oh—that's better!' Lorna groaned half-an-hour later as she eased off her shoes and lay down on the bed. 'It's that terrible jet-lag—God, I hate flying!'

'Well, I'm feeling just great,' Beth said, unpacking her case. 'I must ring Harry and tell him that we've arrived.'

'Fine,' Lorna yawned. 'I'll just have a shower and then a short nap. If you feel like it, how about asking Harry to join us for dinner?'

'That's a great idea. But maybe he won't be able to make it?'

Lorna laughed. 'I think you'll find that he manages to get here—somehow!'

Her confident assurance was rewarded later that day as she and Beth sat having a drink in the oak-panelled cocktail bar. Punctual to the minute, a tall, fair-haired young man came hurrying across the room, smiling broadly as Beth jumped excitedly to her feet. Lorna studied him carefully as he kissed her sister. Back in New York, when Beth had first told her about Harry, she had formed the impression of someone very young and immature. She was surprised, therefore, to find that although he was certainly young, he carried himself with a well-bred confidence; his blue eyes sparkling down at Beth being the only faint resemblance to his cousin, Alex. None of that fatal, charming attraction, she thought with relief. She had been worried that Harry would have inherited some Lothario-like, family trait, but he seemed to be a nice boy, and Beth wouldn't have to worry about her husband straying after every girl he met—not like the poor woman who was foolish enough to marry Alex!

'This is my sister, Lorna,' Beth said as Harry turned to shake her hand.

'Hello, Lorna.' He smiled. 'Beth's told me so much about you. My family and I are so pleased that you could manage to come over and stay with us.'

Top marks for manners, she thought, smiling back at him and remembering the battle he had fought with his family. 'I don't think you'll be surprised to hear that I, too, have heard a great deal about you!' He coloured at her words, grinning sheepishly at Beth, who held his hand, looking relaxed and happy.

Towards the end of dinner, Harry turned to Lorna and asked if he could take Beth on to a nightclub.

'My dear Harry,' she grinned, 'I realise that I'm long in the tooth, but I'm hardly an ancient chaperon! You can both dance the night away as far as I'm concerned. I must say,' she added, looking around at the heavy dark panelling and the opaque, mirrored screens which divided up the dining room, 'this place is really very charming, but not exactly my idea of an exciting venue for young people of your age. It looks more like pictures of the old Trans-Siberian Railway, or maybe a sedate gentleman's club.'

'No ... r-really!' Harry stuttered, pink with embarrassment. 'I didn't mean that you were old. I mean, you—you're really beautiful . . .' He was rescued by Beth, who laughed and said that her sister was only teasing him.

'I meant what I said,' he stoutly insisted. 'I was talking to my cousin in New York the other day. Telling him about you both coming over to stay with us, and all that sort of thing. Anyway, he said that Beth's sister was the most lovely woman he'd ever seen—and he was quite right!'

'Thank you for the compliment.' Lorna tried to school her face into a non-committal smile as an apprehensive lump seemed to have settled in her stomach, and she very much feared it wasn't due to the creamy pudding. Of course Harry was bound to tell Alex about their visit—why on earth hadn't she worked that out for herself? Not that it mattered, she hurriedly assured herself. His cousin was in New York and as far as she knew, had every intention of staying there. Pray God he does, she thought. Beth's visit to the family home was going to be tricky enough, without the addition of its owner! Although Alex was certainly never going to want to see her again after their last meeting, was he?

Lorna waved good night to Beth and Harry, thankfully returning upstairs to the suite and crawling into bed. Scarcely had her head touched the pillow, than she fell immediately into a deep, dreamless sleep. Awoken the next morning by the arrival of the early morning tea tray, she sat up rubbing her eyes as Beth, who seemed as fresh as a daisy, poured out the hot liquid.

'Did you get any sleep at all?' Lorna asked with a yawn.

'Not much!' Beth grinned. 'We went to one or two places—I can't remember any of the names I'm afraid—and then we went for a long walk. It was so romantic in the moonlight—you've no idea!' she sighed happily. 'Do you like Harry?'

Lorna glanced quickly at Beth's anxious face. 'Of course I do. I think that he's going to be perfect for you,' she assured her sister. 'He strikes me as kind and considerate and what our father would, in his old-fashioned way, have undoubtedly called, "a gentleman".'

'Oh, I'm so glad! I wasn't really worried, of course, but ...' she smiled at Lorna's sceptical expression. 'Anyway, he was terribly impressed with you!'

'Impressions—that reminds me!' She swung her legs out of bed. 'We'll have to get our skates on. Since we're expected down at the stately pile tomorrow for tea, we haven't much time to do all our shopping.'

'Shopping? Whatever for?'

Lorna sighed, and went over to pour herself another cup of tea. 'Darling, if you think that your clothes are going to be suitable for the English countryside, you've got another think coming! This isn't New York, and I'll bet every dollar I've got that Oakeley Park isn't centrally heated, or not up to the temperature we're used to, anyway. So, warm underwear is a must—and that's just for starters!'

'Oh, no!'

'Well, you can freeze if you want to, but I don't recommend it!' Lorna looked at her sister's mulish expression. 'OK—you tell me what you're going to wear out for a walk, when it looks as if it's going to rain, hmm?'

'Well, I've got a perfectly good raincoat . . .'

'That one in bright day-glo pink . . .? Fantastic! Just the perfect colour to frighten the sheep, or whatever! And on your feet . . .?' She looked quizzically at Beth, who merely shrugged. 'Look, you've decided to marry your Harry and live in the country,' she said patiently. 'You'll have a wonderful life, but let's face it—you're going to be walking through an awful lot of mud! What's more, if you're worried about how Harry's family will take to you, believe me those "hip" clothes of yours will go down like a lead balloon! So, just place yourself in my hands and I'll guarantee that Harry's mother will think that you're the bee's knees, OK?'

Beth hesitated, and then smiled ruefully. 'Sorry. I forgot for a moment that clothes are your business, and you must know what you're talking about.'

'Are you sure we're not overdoing it?' Beth asked some hours later as she and Lorna sipped a reviving drink of champagne in the pink-and-gold surroundings of the Ritz Hotel. 'I mean, all those boring skirts and cashmere sweaters—I've got a feeling that if I ever get lost in a field, my camouflage will be so perfect that no one would know I was there!'

'I know what you mean, but you'll find I'm right!' Lorna said with a laugh. 'Now, we've only got to buy your wellington boots, and then we're done.'

'Good Lord! What are they?'

'Familiarly known as "gum-boots", they're large, clumping boots . . .' she smiled at the look of horror on Beth's face.

'I'm rapidly going off the thought of my new life,' Beth said, staring gloomily down at the rising bubbles in her glass. 'And what are you going to wear when we're at Oakeley Park?'

'Oh, I think I ought to play the part of the sophisticated New Yorker, don't you? Lying around all day, dressed in scarlet sequins and complaining about the plumbing. They'll be so relieved that you're not like me, that they are sure to welcome you with open arms!'

'You're kidding?'

'Yes, you idiot, of course I am!' Lorna said as Beth sagged with relief. 'And stop worrying! All we've done today is to make sure that the first impression Harry's family has of you, is that you are going to fit into their way of life. Once they are reassured about that, they simply won't notice when you start wearing your old jeans, OK?'

The following day after lunch Lorna took delivery of a hired car and they set off towards Oxfordshire. She had quite deliberately decided not to accept Harry's offer to come up and collect them from the hotel, so that they could drive around the countryside, without needing to rely on Harry or some other member of his family. It would also mean that she could easily leave Oakeley Park as soon as she had made sure that Beth had settled down happily. Leaving the outskirts of London, Lorna eventually found herself travelling up the M40 motorway, surrounded on either side by wide expanses of green fields. Beth was sitting very quietly beside her, her eyes on the scenery and her mind quite obviously elsewhere. It was going to be tough on her sister, of course. Plunging straight into a houseful of strangers was never easy at the best of times, and certainly far more difficult when the people she would be meeting were likely to be viewing her with critical eyes.

'How are you feeling?' she asked, glancing sideways.

'Fine,' Beth's voice sounded nervous. 'Just a bit tired, that's all.'

Lorna didn't suppose that Beth had slept very well last night and neither, for that matter, had she. Despite the three thousand or so miles between them, she still found her nights torturously disturbed by thoughts of Alex. Talking sternly to herself, and trying her hardest to think of other matters, seemed to have no effect at all. His tall lean figure seemed to haunt her dreams, and if it wasn't too ridiculous to contemplate, she could almost imagine that she was falling in love with him. Not that she was, of course—to do anything so stupid would be an unmitigated disaster! Alex clearly didn't even know the meaning of the verb: 'to love'. Somehow, she was just going to have to stagger through this difficult period of her life when, by some terrible quirk of fate, it appeared that she had become enmeshed and entangled by what she could only call a wild, mad infatuation. Surely, the vision of his handsome, tanned face, which seemed to totally fill her mind to the exclusion of all else, was bound to wither and die eventually? She could only hope and pray that it would happen soon.

Thanks to the directions Harry had given Beth for the final part of their journey, they found themselves driving through a small village before turning in through imposing stone gateposts, and on down a long, tree-lined drive.

'I hope this is the right place?' Beth murmured quietly, trying to peer through the trees for some sign of the house. 'Harry's map was very clear, but ... Oh, my goodness!' she exclaimed as Lorna negotiated a hump-backed stone bridge between two lakes, and they caught their first sight of the house. 'It—it's a bit grand, isn't it?' she turned to Lorna, who had stopped the car and was looking at the large Palladian mansion with raised eyebrows.

'Yes, those four, huge pillars are rather imposing, I suppose,' Lorna said carelessly, determined not to be overawed by the enormous, grey stone building, with its long flight of steps up to the entrance portico. 'The heating bills must be horrendous!' she added with a slight laugh as she started up the car, driving down over the gravel and coming to a halt beside the stone steps.

Harry had obviously been on the outlook for them, throwing open the large double front doors and running down the steps. 'I thought you'd never come!' he exclaimed, enveloping Beth in a huge hug. 'Don't worry about your suitcases,' he said to Lorna, 'Simpson will see to those. Come along, I'm dying for you both to meet the family.'

Beth cast one scared look at her sister, before she was towed swiftly up the steps by Harry, Lorna following slowly in her wake. Exactly who Simpson was she had no idea, but undoubtedly all would become clear in time. Entering the large entrance hall, which seemed to be full of barking dogs, it took her some time to sort everyone out. A tall, imposing-looking man in a black jacket and dark striped trousers, who seemed to want to take her coat, announced himself as Simpson, the butler. The dogs calmed down eventually, enough for her to see that they amounted to three black labradors and two elderly grey-and-white terriers; while she assumed that the thin, middle-aged woman with faded, wispy hair, who was limply shaking her hand, must be Harry's mother.

'Did you have a good journey . . .? You must be cold . . . Please see to tea, Simpson . . .' Mrs Kendall talked in small gasps, gesturing vaguely in the air as she did so, and stopping every now and then to absentmindedly pin up another stray lock of hair.

Harry proceeded to take charge, leading the way into what he referred to as the family sitting room. 'The drawing room is much too cold at this time of year,' he said, going over to kick the logs smouldering in a grate below the carved marble mantlepiece. 'We'll have tea in a moment. How was the journey?'

'Oh it was fine,' Beth assured him with sparkling eyes. Lorna noticed that her sister was looking confident and radiantly happy; clearly she wouldn't be nervous as long as Harry was around.

'Do sit down, Miss Grant,' Mrs Kendall spoke from behind her shoulder. 'Such terrible weather we've been having . . . all that rain, you know . . .'

Lorna moved to sit down on a dusky pink couch by the fire, looking about the room as she tried to fend off the terriers who had jumped up beside her, and were trying to lick her face. She didn't like yappy small dogs, and certainly not ones that were as smelly as these two.

'Come here, darlings,' Harry's mother said, lowering herself down beside Lorna and gathering the terriers on to her lap. 'Such adorable little things, aren't they?' she added, beaming down at the animals.

Lorna far preferred the labradors who had rushed into the room and thrown themselves down in front of the fire, but clearly the path towards gaining Mrs Kendall's approval lay in admiring the horrid little beasts. 'They're sweet,' she said as enthusiastically as she could, 'and this is a lovely room.'

'Do you like it?' Harry's mother looked about her vaguely. 'My nephew, Alex, had it redecorated last year. Well, "restoration", he called it . . . I told him at the time that he should have saved his money . . .' she sighed wearily. 'Still, it is his home . . . and I'm just a poor widow-woman, after all.'

Lorna blinked slightly, her expert eye noticing that

the 'poor widow-woman' was wearing an expensively cut tweed suit over a pure silk blouse, her thin hands heavy with diamond rings. Obviously the word 'poor' had a different meaning in this house, she thought, admiring the pale green silk-covered walls and elaborately carved, huge mirror. Set opposite the two long windows, it reflected the dying rays of the late afternoon sun and cast a shimmering glow over the fine mahoghany furniture. 'It really is a beautiful room,' she was saying again as Mrs Kendall raised her head and looked over her shoulder.

'Ah, here is Simpson with the tea, at last . . . and dear Augusta, too ... I don't think you've met my daughter?' the older woman murmured as a tall blonde entered the room.

'Hello, Ma.' The girl bent over to kiss her mother's faded cheek, before looking down at Lorna with startled eyes. 'Good God! No wonder Harry chucked poor old Lavinia—he never told us you were so good-looking!'

'Thank you,' Lorna said with a dry smile, 'but I'm afraid that you're talking to the wrong person! I'm Lorna Grant, and that's my sister, Beth, over there,' she nodded towards the young couple chatting in a corner of the room

'Whoops—sorry!' the girl grinned. 'I forgot that there were going to be two of you staying with us. I'd better go over and try and say the right thing this time, or Harry will never forgive me! And do hurry up with that tea, Ma, I'm starving!' she added over her shoulder as she strode across the room.

Mrs Kendall showed the two sisters into their adjoining bedrooms after tea was over, disjointedly murmuring something about dinner at eight o'clock as she hurried away. A moment later, Beth knocked on Lorna's door and came in.

'How do you like your future mother-in-law?' Lorna asked carefully.

'Well, she's . . .' Beth hesitated, and then giggled. 'She seems a bit funny! Still,' she added quickly, 'I've hardly had time to get to know her yet.'

'I thought Harry's sister, Augusta, seemed very nice,' Lorna said, deciding that there was little point in saying any more about Mrs Kendall, whom she privately thought would prove to be a real pain in the neck.

'Yes, she is nice, isn't she?' Beth said enthusiastically. 'She asked me to call her "Gussie" straight away, and she seems awfully fond of Harry. I know!' she laughed. 'You were right, all along. It was silly of me to worry.'

'In your shoes, I would have been just as nervous,' Lorna assured her. 'These bedrooms are pretty, aren't they?' she added, looking around the room which was decorated in pale blue and white.

'Yes, Harry said that Alex has been slowly redecorating the whole house, room by room, over the last five years. What I don't quite understand,' Beth frowned, 'is why they got so het-up about Harry having to marry a wealthy girl. They seem to be living very comfortably here, don't they?'

'Well, I expect this huge building takes a lot of looking after, and I imagine that the wage bill for the servants can't be peanuts, either. However, that's not your problem. You and Harry will be comfortably tucked up in your farm house, and if Alex ever runs out of money,' Lorna added grimly, 'he will undoubtedly soon be able to find himself a rich wife!'

'I wish you liked him,' Beth said quietly. 'He's been so kind to both Harry and myself . . .'

'Take no notice of me,' Lorna said quickly. 'I'm just tired, that's all. Now, Mrs Kendall did say eight o'clock for dinner, didn't she?'

'Yes. You were quite right about the heating, by the way. Harry said to be sure and wear something long and warm!'

'Thanks for the warning,' Lorna laughed. 'You'd better choose the long, green dress,' she told Beth as she left the room.

Exploring her new surroundings, Lorna discovered a small bathroom leading off the bedroom, prettily decorated in a matching shade of pale blue. Feeling somewhat tired from the tensions of the day, she decided to run a bath, slipping into the warm water with a deep sigh of content.

An hour later she was dressed and sorting through her jewel box, trying to decide what earrings to wear, when Beth came in. 'You look great,' Lorna said, gazing with approval at the green wool jersey dress which blended so well with her sister's auburn curls. Its fitted bodice emphasised her soft curves and slim waist, below which the unpressed pleats of the skirt fell away to the ground.

'You look pretty stunning, yourself!' Beth told Lorna, whose tall figure was wrapped in a slinky, figure-hugging black silk jersey dress.

'For heaven's sake, I've had this old thing for years,' Lorna murmured as she leant forward to clip on a pair of topaz-and-diamond earrings, the last present she'd had from her father before he died. Checking quickly in the mirror on the heavy, loose coil of hair pinned at the nape of her neck, she gave herself a final spray of perfume and turned around to face Beth. 'OK, that's it. We'd better go downstairs, and let's hope that your Harry is heavy-handed with the gin bottle—I could certainly do with a strong drink!' she murmured, leading the way down the marble staircase, across the large hall and into the room where they had met for tea.

While Harry fixed them a drink, Lorna breathed with relief to note that she and Beth were dressed similarly to his mother and Gussie. With Beth chatting happily away to Harry and his sister, it was left to Lorna to try and make some sort of conversation with Mrs Kendall.

Not an easy task, she thought grimly, deciding that she had never met anyone who found life such a trial. It appeared that the servants were always giving trouble, the butcher constantly delivered the wrong cuts of meat, the weather had been so terrible ... the list seemed endless! Desperately hunting around in her mind for something to take the older woman's mind off her problems, Lorna's thoughts were suddenly interrupted by the three black labradors springing to their feet and barking loudly as they raced out of the room.

'Who can be calling at this time of night?' Gussie said, before giving a shriek of delight and running across the room to throw her arms about the tall, dark figure standing in the doorway. '*Alex!* You never told us you were coming!'

'Cool it, Gussie—give me a chance to breathe!' Alex laughed, kissing her cheek. 'Hello, Aunt Sophie. We seem to have visitors, I see.'

Lorna had almost fainted with shock at Alex's entrance, her body suddenly turned to stone, just like one of the marble statues out in the large hall. She couldn't seem to move, trying to focus her glazed eyes as he walked over to greet Beth before turning towards her.

'Good evening, Lorna,' he drawled. 'How nice to see you again.'

'I—I ...' she croaked, her knuckles whitening as her fingers tightened about her glass in a vice-like grip.

'You're looking rather pale. Are you sure that you're feeling all right?' Alex asked, his sympathetic words belied by the sardonic, glinting amusement in his blue eyes.

Lorna glared at him with loathing as she desperately tried to pull herself together. 'What—what are you doing here ...?' she hissed angrily.

'My dear girl!' He lifted one dark brow. 'It is my home, you know! And besides which, I hardly feel that

I have to account to you for my actions, do you?' he murmured with silky menace.

Despite all her efforts, Lorna couldn't prevent a deep blush from covering her face as she realised just what a fool she had made of herself. The stinging reproof delivered with such cool finesse, had been meant to hurt—and it did—leaving her feeling as if she had been violently slapped in the face.

The blue eyes regarding her so intently, darkened momentarily and then Alex turned abruptly away. 'I'd better go off and get changed. Come and chat to me while I'm dressing, Harry, and then I can catch up with all the news.' He put his arm around his cousin's shoulder and led him out of the room.

Later, as she sat fiddling with her food, and trying to ignore Mrs Kendall's perpetual moaning, Lorna glanced through her eyelashes down the table at Alex, who was laughing and joking with his cousins. He seemed almost a different man in his own home environment. Far more relaxed than she had ever seen him, as he leaned back holding a glass of wine in his hands and smiling at something Gussie was saying.

Since returning to the sitting room, just as dinner was announced by Simpson, he had conspicuously ignored Lorna, although he had been charm itself to Beth. God, I really hate him, she fumed, tearing her eyes away from the tanned, smiling face. What on earth was she to do now? Wild plans for escape filled her mind, only to be discarded as she faced the dreadful fact that she was stuck. She'd promised Beth that she would stay at Oakeley Park for a few days, and if she went back on her word now, how on earth could she possibly explain why?

CHAPTER SEVEN

LORNA sat up in the bath, wringing out her sponge and attempting to wipe away the flood of tears running down her cheeks. Thank God none of her friends could see her now. That Lorna Grant, who had always been known for her cool self-possession, could be sitting here blubbing like a baby ... they'd never believe it! She must pull herself together, she simply must! Leaning over the side of the bath she extracted some tissues from her make-up bag and blew her nose fiercely, before lying back in the warm water and staring blindly through the clouds of steam as she tried to work out what on earth she was going to do.

There was no doubt that it had been one of the worst days of her life, one way and another. Certainly she couldn't remember having felt such a heavy weight of depression, not since Carlo's death, anyway. At least when her father had died, she had been so busy both trying to clear up the mess and also keeping up Beth's spirits, that she had had little time to think of her own misery. Very different from her present situation, stuck here in this damned stately home. Despite the fact that there was a perfectly good hired car sitting in Oakeley Park's palatial garage, it was about as much use to her as a sick headache. Her first impulse to jump in and drive as far away as possible, was a complete non-starter; because that would mean leaving Beth to face everything on her own, and she really couldn't do that, could she?

Lorna wearily closed her eyes. She was still feeling tired to death, despite having had a long, exhausted sleep this afternoon. Maybe it was because she had spent the whole of last night tossing and turning in her bed, wondering why Alex should have decided to make such a dramatic and sudden appearance. She had managed to stagger through dinner, stuck beside that awful Mrs Kendall and her constant whining—how Harry and Gussie put up with it she had no idea! And it was only her pride that had kept her going, when they all adjourned to the sitting room after the meal. However foul Alex was, she was damned if she was going to let him know—more that she had already— just how shattering she had found his sudden reappearance in her life.

She tried to comfort herself with the thought that it wasn't surprising she had been upset. Following all they had said to each other, and especially after the way Alex had stormed out of her apartment after trying to make love to her, she had assumed that he would have taken the greatest care not to come within a hundred miles of her. Instead of which, he'd just strolled into the house as cool as a cucumber, mentally pistol-whipped her around the head, and had then proceeded to enjoy himself laughing and joking with his cousins—what a swine the man was!

Waking up at the crack of dawn this morning, she'd lain for a long time trying to decide what to do, without coming to any firm conclusion. Mrs Kendall hadn't bothered to say what time breakfast was served, but by eight o'clock Lorna knew that if she didn't have a cup of coffee, she'd die! Swiftly getting dressed in a pair of black linen slacks, with a long, black cashmere cardigan over a white silk shirt, she tip-toed out of her room, anxious not to wake her sister, undoubtedly fast asleep next door. Hesitating for a moment, Lorna decided that she didn't give a hoot if she scandalised the entire family and servants by being up too early. 'To hell with them!' she muttered, making her way down the long flight of stairs in search of liquid refreshment.

Almost the first person she met was Simpson, the butler, who was directing the progress of a maid, busily scrubbing on her hands and knees the black and white marble floor of the hall. Explaining her dilemma, he smiled and directed her across the hall where, he assured her, she would find that breakfast was awaiting her pleasure. 'And coffee, too, of course, madam!' he added, before moving stately off about his business.

Just about to enter the room, she heard the sound of voices and caught a glimpse through the open door of Alex's tall figure seated at the head of the long, gleaming mahogany table. Nervously backing away, she realised it was too late as he called out for her to come and join them. Slowly retracing her steps, she found that 'them' consisted of Gussie, Harry and, of course, Alex.

'Well, well, if it isn't the glamorous Lorna Grant! I thought lovely ladies like you lay in bed all day, hmm?'

She gritted her teeth. The poisonous swine was a photographer, and therefore he knew very well that when she was working, she would normally get up very early indeed.

'Don't be so foul, Alex,' Gussie said, looking up startled at the sarcastic tone in his voice and swiftly coming to Lorna's aid. 'He's always simply horrid first thing in the morning, I'd just ignore him if I was you.'

'Oh, I shall,' Lorna said, going over to the long sideboard and pouring herself a cup of coffee. 'Not that I would have known if you hadn't told me. Your cousin strikes me as behaving in his usual, utterly charming manner. I can't wait to see what improvement he's likely to exhibit during the day!'

Responding like that, as she freely admitted privately to herself, had been a mistake. The strong lines of Alex's face tightened in anger, his blue eyes becoming hard as flintstones and glinting dangerously at her down the length of the table. However, it seemed that he chose to ignore her words as she sat down next to Gussie, turning to Harry and discussing some work to be done on the estate.

'I do like your sister, she's going to be perfect for Harry, isn't she?' Gussie's words interrupted Lorna's sombre thoughts.

'Yes, I'm sure they're going to be very happy,' Lorna smiled gratefully at the blonde girl. 'I may not be able to stay very long here, and so I do hope that if she gets in a muddle, you'll be able to help her out. England is very different from America,' she added.

'Sure, I'll be pleased to help in any way I can,' Gussie said. 'I'm taking a few weeks off work, anyway.'

'You don't live here all the time?' Lorna queried.

'Good lord, no! Mother would drive me up the wall in five seconds flat!' Gussie laughed. 'No, I live in London, sharing a grotty flat with two other girls I met at school. Rotten old Alex said I would be hopeless in an office and sent me off to do a Cordon Bleu cookery course. Actually,' she confided with a grin, 'my cooking is best described as "Cordon Blah"! Still, I've joined up with another girl and we do lunches for some firms in the City.'

'Do you enjoy it? Cooking I mean?'

Gussie shrugged. 'It's all right, I suppose. Except when it gets in the way of my social life! Not that I've got much of a one at the moment—that's why I'm comfort eating,' she said, reaching out for another piece of toast.

'It doesn't seem to be doing you any harm!' Lorna laughed, looking at Gussie's slim, almost flat-chested figure.

'That's the problem. I had this really super boyfriend. He looked absolutely divine and I was mad on him. Then he met another girl, an awful redhead with a forty-inch bust—and that was that! I can see I shall have to get some heavily padded bras, or hope that

Rupert will find me someone smashing—isn't life a drag!'

Lorna smiled, deciding that she liked Gussie very much indeed. 'Rupert is your brother, I take it?'

'Yes, we're twins actually. He's at Sandhurst at the moment, playing at being a soldier. It looks as if he will be on duty and not able to get away to join us up here for Easter; he's awfully fed up about it.'

'Are you very close?'

'Quite. More so when we were younger, of course. Hey—wait for me, Harry!' Gussie called out, jumping to her feet. 'I'll see you at lunch, I expect. 'Bye,' she said quickly to Lorna, before running after her brother's disappearing figure.

There was a long silence as Lorna stared down at her cup, wondering how on earth she could get out of the room without another nasty exchange between herself and Alex. She had been fully aware of his searching glances down the table as she had talked to Gussie, and now cautiously raising her head, she saw that he was leaning back in his chair and regarding her with an enigmatic expression.

'I—er . . .' he cleared his throat. 'We do seem to rub each other up the wrong way, don't we, Lorna? However, it seems a pity if we should let our—er—past encounters spoil the atmosphere, especially as far as Beth and Harry are concerned. Don't you agree?'

He uses his charm like a weapon, she thought, suddenly finding herself growing hot and reeling under the impact of his engaging smile. It seemed to take the most enormous effort for her to maintain her cool expression in the face of such blandishment.

'Yes, I agree,' she replied warily.

'I knew you would,' he murmured, and Lorna seethed with a fierce longing to slap the complacent expression from his face. 'So, I suggest that it might be a good idea if we should appear to have buried our differences,' he added. 'To at least maintain the fiction that we are friends, hmm?'

What the hell ... Lorna shrugged. He was right, of course. If they didn't make an effort, the tension between them would soon start to upset the family, and Beth too, of course. Still, she wasn't going to let the arrogant bastard have it all his own way.

'Do you think we could have a truce?' he asked.

'Why not, Alex, *dear*,' she cooed, giving him a brilliant smile.

'I'm so glad—Lorna, *darling*,' he countered swiftly, before throwing back his head and roaring with laughter.

Lorna stared down at the remains of her cold coffee, feeling as miserable as sin. It seemed, despite the so-called truce, that somehow war had just been declared, and from the way that dreadful man was laughing, it looked as if she was likely to be the first casualty.

'Cheer up! I promise not to tease you any more, in fact ...' he paused, tilting his head as he listened to some sound. 'Oh God! Aunt Sophie is coming, and if there is one thing I can't stand at any time, let alone the first thing in the morning, it's having to listen to her whining about life.' He rose to his feet and strode swiftly towards a door at the end of the room. 'Come on—hurry up, Lorna. You might hate me, but I can assure you that you'll have a far worse time if you stay here with my aunt!'

What he said was so patently true, that she obediently stood up and went over to join him, trying to ignore the fact that he firmly captured one of her hands in his as he led them swiftly away down the corridor.

'Where—where are we going?' she asked.

'Well away from my dear aunt, of course. Actually, I may as well give you a short tour of the house—if you'd like to see over it, that is?'

'I suppose I might as well,' she muttered ungraciously. 'I believe you've been doing quite a lot of restoration.'

'Yes, the place had got into a terrible state. With ten thousand acres to support the house, there was no reason why it should have done. It was my father's fault, really. He was only interested in breeding racehorses, and didn't notice that the house was crumbling down about his ears. Almost the first thing I did when I inherited the property, was to sell the horses. Ah, here we are. This is where I retire to get away from everyone.' He laughed. 'Principally my aunt, of course.'

They had been travelling down long corridors and now Alex led her, his hand still firmly holding hers, into a charming small room which he informed her had previously been the boudoir of the house. 'The ladies used to come here and do their sewing—hundreds of years ago the poor dears had nothing else to do with themselves. They must have led hideously boring lives, don't you think?'

Lorna was having difficulty in thinking anything. Alex's tall figure standing so close to her seemed to be having a devastating effect on her breathing, while her heart was beating so loudly that she was convinced he could hear the rapid tattoo. She couldn't seem to move, either, her legs turned to jelly as his thumb gently stroked the soft inner skin of her wrist.

'Yes—yes, it's a lovely room,' she managed to say at last, deliberately not meeting his eyes as she looked around at her surroundings. 'I can see that you might want to be alone in here, but—but if you don't care for your aunt, why do you let her live in your house?'

'Ah, well,' he laughed, but whether at her words, or because she had finally managed to withdraw her hand from his, she wasn't sure. 'Mainly for my cousins' sake. My Uncle Duncan, Aunt Sophie's husband, did in fact leave her very well off when he died. But I'm afraid that although she spends any amount of money on herself, she couldn't be relied upon to see that her children were properly educated, or looked after in every other way. They were quite young when their father died,' he explained, 'and so I felt fairly responsible. Letting my aunt come and live here meant I could keep an eye on Harry and the twins, and see that they weren't neglected. Aunt Sophie is as merry as a cricket at not having to spend any of her money on living expenses, which is the real reason why she was so keen for Harry to marry that rich girl, Lavinia. I'm afraid that my dear aunt is one of those people who says, "Oh, no, I'm not hungry"—and then takes the largest slice of the chocolate cake!'

Lorna found herself laughing at his analogy and impressed, despite herself, with his kind concern for his cousins.

'Of course, the arrangement drives my mother up the wall! She and my aunt cordially detest each other, my mama deeply resents her sister-in-law's assumption that I shall never marry, and that Harry will inherit the estate. But we've discussed all that before, haven't we?' he laughed. 'That was the first time—but, alas, not the last—when you told me to "get lost"!'

'Where—where does your mother live?' Lorna said hurriedly, walking over to the window and trying to hide her flushed cheeks as she gazed out at the sheep on the broad acres of the park.

'Oh, she married again soon after my father died, and lives in Paris. She apparently rang up last week and announced that she was coming to stay for a few days, so you may well meet her. She's married to a rich Frenchman—now he really is a charming smoothie— and he won't mind you calling him "loverboy" one little bit, in fact he'll love it!'

Oh God! Alex really was extracting his pound of flesh today, wasn't he? Lorna leant her hot face against a cold pane of glass, suddenly feeling unutterably depressed. Knowing that her words in the past had cut through his apparently impervious self-possession didn't seem to help matters, somehow. Before she could think of an adequate reply, he had taken her limp hand and was leading her through the door, up a flight of stairs and into a long gallery.

'This is the oldest part of the house, and what I always think of as the rogues' gallery,' he explained.

'Are—are the portraits all members of your family?'

Alex didn't seem to notice the breathlessness of her voice. 'They're mostly of my grandmother's family, actually. We Kendalls are very much newcomers, you know. My grandfather was the son of a Scottish minister, who left home to come down to England and made a fortune in munitions during the First World War. He and my grandmother fell madly in love when she was only eighteen. This was her house, and she was the only child of Earl Oakeley—a scandalous rake if one believes only half the gossip of the times. When she ran off to marry my grandfather, the old Earl cut her off with the proverbial shilling, only relenting when she produced my father ... and here we all are, today.'

'I thought that ...' Lorna hesitated.

'You thought that we'd been here since the Domesday Book? I'm afraid not!' he laughed. 'The shocking truth is that my grandfather stumped up one hundred thousand pounds to buy his title from old Lloyd George, when the Prime Minister was selling peerages in an effort to raise funds for the Liberal party—so you see, we aren't really very grand at all! Although my mother still hangs on to her title—she says the French are terrible snobs!—she really ought to call herself plain Mrs Fournier. Does that make you feel any better?'

'I—I don't know what you mean?'

Alex gave a heavy sigh. 'I do wish, my dear Lorna,

that you would try and see me as I really am: just a very ordinary man, who happens to take pictures for a living, that's all. I—I had hoped that you might come to understand that I love my huge, draughty old house, and that I fully intend to settle down here with my future wife and have lots of children—despite Aunt Sophie's hopes to the contrary! Is it so surprising?'

'No—no of course not,' she muttered. 'But I don't see that it—it has anything . . .'

'Anything to do with you?'

'Stop finishing my sentences!' she snapped, finding that despite the spaciousness of the long gallery, she was suddenly feeling claustrophobic. Alex was still somehow holding on to her hand and now, as he leaned forward to tuck a stray lock of her long blonde hair behind her ear, the touch of his warm fingers was causing her to shiver and tremble like a leaf in the wind.

Gently pulling her towards him, he lowered his dark head to softly brush her cheek with his lips. 'My God,' he breathed, 'you smell wonderful . . .! What is it?'

'My . . . my p-perfume . . .?' She was totally confused by his question and far more concerned about her legs, which seemed as weak as water and about to collapse at any moment. 'It . . . it's c-called "*Sheherazade*",' she gasped as his tongue began to sensuously explore the outer shell of her ear.

His arms closed about her as faint with dizziness she swayed against the firm support of his hard body. 'If only I could have the delicious pleasure of spending One Thousand and One Nights with you,' he whispered, lowering his head until his mouth was poised only a fraction above her own, before moving to slowly and delicately sketch the outline of her lips.

Lorna could feel all her remaining resistance dissolving as the pressure of his lips slowly and gently increased. She wasn't conscious of the exact moment when the soft, beguiling caress of his mouth became a kiss of possessive, scorching intensity. From the instant his lips touched hers, they had torn down all her carefully erected barriers, her body weak and helpless as she surrendered to the passionate response he was demanding.

All reality seemed to have been swept away and she was only aware of the erotic brush of his hand on her rounded breasts, causing her to tremble with heated excitement, and of the thighs pressing so closely against hers betraying evidence of his own arousal. Her fingers buried themselves convulsively in the dark, thick texture of his hair, her body fusing with his to become one entity and aware only of an overwhelming, driving force deep inside her clamouring for release. His burning lips demanded her total submission, his kiss deepening until she was hardly able to breathe, before he slowly began to release the pressure.

A shaft of brilliant morning sunshine blazed in her eyes as her fluttering lashes slowly opened, her vision filled with Alex's tanned face only inches away from her own. His mouth was curved into a crooked, wry smile, his blue eyes glittering darkly down, boring into hers as if intent on an answer to some inscrutable question.

Lorna could feel her face begin to burn as a tide of deep crimson flooded over her cheeks. Oh God—she'd let it happen again! Despite everything she knew about this man, she'd fallen like a ripe plum just as soon as he'd touched her. And as for him . . .? He *knew* his power over her—what else could that smile mean, but self-satisfaction at demonstrating once more his mastery of her emotions?

Tearing herself out of his loose, encircling arms, she tottered on legs that felt like cotton wool towards a wide window seat. Sinking down, she buried her face in her hands for a moment, desperately trying to hide his face and figure from her view. Still trying to collect herself, she felt the cushioned seat move as he came over to sit down beside her, his arms going about her miserably hunched figure. For one mad, insane moment she allowed herself to relax against him, to savour the strength of his hard body and the total security of his embrace as he gently stroked her long hair and murmured soft words of endearment. Then the bright sunlight beating down on the side of her face brought reality flooding back, and she jerked herself out of his arms as if she had been stung.

'For—for heaven's sake—leave me alone!' she cried, her body trembling as if in the grip of a raging fever.

'Lorna! You don't understand . . .'

'Yes . . . yes I do!' she countered quickly, somehow managing to find the strength to get to her feet. 'I—I understand only too damn well—that's the trouble!'

'If you would only let me explain, I . . .'

Lorna brushed a distracted hand across her brow. 'Oh God, Alex—cut it out, will you? Save all your pretty speeches for the girls who'll appreciate them, OK?' She shook her head wearily. 'I—I'm not blaming you, it's all my own damn fault. At my age you'd think I'd know better, wouldn't you?' she gave an unhappy, shaky laugh and turned to go.

'Running away again, Lorna?' he said from behind her, his voice harsh and strained. 'Don't try and fool yourself that running away from me and the truth will solve anything, because it won't.'

'My God!' she spun around angrily, her long gold hair flowing about her head. 'You're really incredible! "The truth." OK, I'll give you the Goddamn truth—and then maybe you'll leave me alone. The sad, pathetic truth is that you are one hell of a sexy guy—and don't you just know it!—who is capable of making me go weak at the knees . . . There—how's that for a confession to *really* make your day! You know, and I know, that unfortunately I seem to be a pushover for your particular brand of sensual charm ...'

'Don't be so damn stupid, Lorna!' he retorted furiously, his face beneath his tan becoming pale with tension.

'Yes—I really am damn stupid to have come within a million miles of you—and I don't need you to tell me that! I ...' She was shivering with tension, unable to control either her tongue or her self-contempt. 'I'm one, big fool—that's what I am. I don't like or approve of anything about you—your reputation, your lifestyle, the incredible arrogance and conceit with which you won't take "no" for an answer ... My God, you're obviously so used to women falling down on the ground in front of you, that you simply can't understand anyone declining the pleasure, can you? And as for ...'

'*That's quite enough!*' Alex shouted, the sound of his angry roar ringing in her ears as she closed her eyes and stood trembling with nervous exhaustion. 'If you weren't a guest in my house, I'd feel very tempted to try and slap some sense into that beautiful head of yours. Don't you think it's about time you stopped reading all those stupid gossip columns? I wouldn't believe any nonsense they wrote about you, not now that I know you—so why be so obstinately blind about me? One fine day,' he ground out bitterly, 'you might actually manage to break out of your mental strait-jacket, and get around to admitting that you're a real live woman, with real live emotional needs and feelings! Unfortunately, when that happy day comes at last, it will be too damn late. Because I, for one, have had just about as much of you as I can take!'

Lorna flinched at the brutal tone in his voice, opening her eyes to see him staring at her with such icy-cold contempt that she almost moaned with pain. Harsh lines etched his still face, which suddenly came to life as his eyes blazed scornfully into hers for a moment before he turned on his heel and strode swiftly away.

Collapsing on to a small chair, she heard the clatter of his footsteps hurrying down the stairs, followed by the bang of a door as he slammed it behind him. How long she sat, rigidly stiff as a statue, she had no idea. Time seemed to have no meaning as the frozen knot of sickness lodged in her stomach gradually spread throughout her body. Wearily rising to her feet she moved slowly through the quiet house, not knowing or caring when she occasionally got lost in the long, deserted corridors. Finally reaching her room, she walked blindly into the bathroom, seeking some aspirin for what was fast becoming a blinding headache.

'I hate him—*I hate him!*' Lorna said aloud to her reflection in the mirror above the basin, hardly recognising the shocked, pale image staring back from dazed, slanting green eyes that called her a liar. She shivered uncontrollably, realising that it didn't matter how hard she rubbed her soft skin, nothing could wash away the inescapable truth: that she was head over heals in love with Alex Kendall.

Wrestling with the painful, mortifying discovery that incredible as it might seem, she loved a man who was only hell-bent on seduction, Lorna stayed in her room all morning, desperately trying to come to terms with what she could only think of as a disaster of unquantifiable magnitude. What on earth was she to do? A question that became a constant refrain running through her brain, and one to which she could find no answer.

The sound of a gong reverberating in the distance made her look down at her watch. It must signal lunch, she realised, amazed that so much time had passed since breakfast. The very last thing she wanted was food, but if she remained up here, sooner or later someone was sure to come and find her. Slowly rising to her feet, her body feeling as though it carried a ton weight, the habits of a lifetime automatically reasserted themselves as she absentmindedly went over to brush her hair and repair her make-up, before slowly trailing down the long marble staircase.

Standing outside the door of the sitting room from within which she could hear voices, she took a deep breath and tried to brace herself for the coming confrontation with Alex. 'Come on—you can do it,' she whispered to herself. The past three years of staring disdainfully through camera lenses, despite anything she might be feeling at the time, must surely count for something? Swallowing convulsively, she opened the door.

'Lorna, where have you been all morning?' Beth smiled at her from a settee where she sat next to Harry. We've been looking all over the place for you.'

'Yes, I . . .' Lorna shrugged. 'I was just exploring the house,' she said, accepting a drink from Harry and grateful to have something to cling to.

'Such a large, draughty house . . . So much work to look after . . .' Mrs Kendall moaned quietly from a chair, her lap covered by a snuffling dog. 'And where is Alex? He must have heard the gong . . . Never any consideration to keep us waiting like this . . . it's too bad . . .'

Despite her own problems, Lorna noticed that Beth had obviously decided to take her cue from Harry, ignoring her future mother-in-law's whining complaints and brightly pointing out that there was still ten minutes to go before lunchtime. Her words were interrupted by a background noise of car doors banging, dogs barking and shrieks of laughter. A moment later, the sitting room door was thrown open by Gussie, followed by a striking looking woman who stood in the entrance and regarded the occupants with an amused, mocking smile.

'Hello, darlings!' she laughed. 'I see I'm just in time for a lovely drink before lunch—didn't we time our arrival well!'

It didn't need Harry's welcoming shout of, 'Aunt Caroline . . .!' for Lorna to realise that Alex's mother had arrived. If she'd only seen the older woman in the street, she would still have known instantly who she was, the resemblance to her son being quite unmistakable. The same dark hair, brilliant blue eyes and charming, smiling mouth were reflected by her son, who entered the room just as she gave Harry a big hug.

'Well, Mother, I see you managed to get here in one piece! Jacques didn't manage to smash your car up this time, I notice!'

'Horrid boy!' Mother and son smiled fondly at each other. 'Poor Jacques always finds driving on the wrong side of the road such a trial! Thank you, Harry, darling,' she murmured, slipping off her dark mink coat as she accepted a drink from her nephew, a collection of wide, heavy gold bracelets tinkling as she raised the glass to her lips.

'Wonderful—I needed that,' Alex's mother murmured before turning around to survey the other occupants of the room. 'Darling Sophie, I see that you still have those nasty, smelly dogs! And . . .*quelle surprise*—who have we here?' She raised an eyebrow as she noticed Beth and Lorna.

'This is Beth Grant, who has just become engaged to Harry,' Alex said, coming over to introduce his mother.

'Pretty child . . .' Lady Caroline murmured, shaking Beth's hand.

'And this is Lorna Grant, Beth's older sister, who is staying with us for a few days.' Alex gazed calmly into Lorna's eyes as he said the words, not showing for an instant that there had been anything between them but the briefest acquaintance, and certainly no trace of the cataclysmic scene upstairs in the long gallery this morning. 'My mother, Lady Caroline Fournier,' he added.

With a herculean effort, Lorna managed to gaze coolly at Alex before turning to smile politely at his mother.

'Oh, but you're a ravishing beauty!' the older woman exclaimed. 'Yes, I can see now why . . .' her words were cut short as laughter could be heard out in the hall. 'Oh darling—I'm sorry . . .' she turned quickly to her son. 'I *know* how you hate me getting involved in your private life, but I really couldn't help it. We bumped into her at the Savoy, and you know Jacques . . .! He insisted on bringing her down, and . . .'

Lorna could feel Alex stiffen beside her as all eyes in the room swivelled to stare at the vision in the doorway. The sculptured perfection of the girl's face, the warm golden skin and midnight black hair arranged in loose curls set over a perfect pocket-Venus shaped figure, almost took Lorna's breath away. She was used to working with outstandingly beautiful women, but she had seldom seen anyone as lovely as the girl who threw her arms open wide and ran into Alex's embrace.

'My darling, *gioia mia!*' she breathed in an entrancing Italian accent as she wound her slim arms about his neck. 'I knew you must be missing me—and so, here I am!' she laughed gaily, nestling within his arms and gazing up adoringly into his face.

'*Bonjour*, Alex. I 'ave brought you a leetle surprise, yes?' A tall, aristocratic grey-haired Frenchman accepted a drink from Harry and beamed at the couple embracing in the centre of the room. 'I told you, my darling,' he said to Lady Caroline, 'that your dear boy would be pleased. Me, I am never wrong in matters of the heart!'

Lorna stood rooted to the floor, knowing without a shadow of a doubt that the feelings tearing at her heart with sharp, venomous claws, were nothing more or less

than an overwhelming surge of pure feminine jealousy.
Feeling faint and almost sick, she turned away to stare
out of the window while she struggled to control her
emotions. Like an animal in pain, she wanted only to
escape to some deep, dark burrow where she could lick
her wounds in secret privacy. But she was given no
opportunity as Mrs Kendall began to shepherd
everyone towards the dining room.

Lunch was a nightmare. Seated beside Alex's French
stepfather, who clearly regarded himself as a lady-
killer, Lorna could only respond to his flirtatious
advances with barely concealed irritation. The whole
focus of her attention, and indeed of everyone else's at
the table, was the vivacious chatter from the Italian girl,
who it appeared was called Luci Borgini. Peering
through her eyelashes at the girl, illuminated by a shaft
of bright midday sun as she laughed and sparkled up at
Alex, Lorna felt unutterably low and depressed. Try as
she might, she could discern no flaw in that perfect
complexion, and certainly neither could Alex. Bending
his head to listen to something Luci was saying, the
strong lines of his tanned cheek portrayed nothing but
delight in her sudden appearance.

'They 'ave been lovers for a long time, I think!' the
Frenchman whispered as he followed the direction of
her eyes. 'You are a beautiful girl, too,' he leered, placing
a groping hand on her knee. Lorna sighed as she
wriggled away, gloomily remembering Alex's words
about his stepfather.

Like all bad dreams, eventually lunch came to an end
and Lorna could make good her escape. Telling Beth
that she had a shattering headache—which was no less
than the truth—she fled upstairs to her room. Swiftly
shutting the door, she had thrown herself across the bed
in a storm of tears and, possibly because of her sleepless
night, had fallen at last into exhausted oblivion.

The cooling water of the bath intruded into her

distracted thoughts, and stepping out to envelop herself in a warm towel, she walked slowly through into her bedroom and sat down in front of the dressing table. God knows what she could possibly do with her face which was looking absolutely appalling—all red and blotchy from weeping in the bath. It would take every ounce of skill she possessed to even look faintly normal for dinner tonight.

At the thought of the coming ordeal, she felt quite sick. How on earth was she going to stagger through the evening? Having to make polite conversation and keep smiling while Alex and his Luci billed and cooed at each other, was more than flesh and blood could stand. Were they together now, making love before dinner ...? Lorna almost fainted at the thought, shivering and trembling as she recalled the abandoned way she had responded to Alex's passionate kiss this morning.

How could she possibly love someone who was so amoral? Who charmed, used and then discarded women without a thought? God knows why—but she did. Once she was in his embrace, the knowledge that he was a charming seducer seemed to mean nothing at all! She moaned aloud as she faced the fact that she didn't care ... She didn't care what he was—or what sort of relationship he had with the Italian girl; the shocking realisation that given the same circumstances again, she was still capable of falling blindly into his arms, left her feeling completely shattered and badly frightened.

CHAPTER EIGHT

LORNA looked up, welcoming the feel of stinging rain on her face. It had been overcast all day, and now the heavens had opened to produce a drenching downpour. She decided that despite becoming wet and bedraggled, she was content to continue trudging across the park, the stormy grey light of the sky admirably suiting her sombre mood.

It was an hour since she, Harry and Beth had started out for a bracing walk after lunch. Harry had shown them around the stables, empty now of the racehorses Alex's father had cared for so deeply. Only three horses remained, contentedly munching their hay and looked after by a wizened old Irishman who looked far too old to carry a bucket, let alone have the strength to clean out the stalls.

'There's only Miss Gussie's hack and Master Alex's two hunters left now. And that's a great pity I'm thinking,' he muttered, sizing up the two sisters very much as he would one of his precious animals. 'You've got the legs for it,' he informed Lorna. 'Would you be wanting a ride now?'

She looked longingly at a bay mare, remembering how mad she had been on riding when she was in her early teens. 'I'm sorry,' she shook her head sadly, 'I simply don't have the right clothes with me. Some other time, maybe,' she added, in an attempt to cushion his obvious disappointment, knowing that there never would be another time for her, not here at Oakeley Park.

Led by Harry, she and Beth went on to explore the old beer house and the equally ancient laundry, before

149

crossing the large courtyard to view the white-tiled, cool expanse of the dairy, last used in Victorian times.

'It's a pity more people can't see such a quaint old place,' Beth remarked idly, trailing her fingers over the large china jugs and wide bowls.

'Alex has often thought about opening the house during the summer,' Harry said. 'You know, letting people come and pay to look around. But he's away a great deal of the year, and since I'm far too busy on the estate, he feels that it would all be a bit much for Mother to manage on her own. However, he'll probably do something about it when he gets married.'

'Is he thinking of marrying Luci?' Beth asked, her eyes sparkling with interest and her mind very obviously on weddings.

'Well, I don't know what he's thinking about—one never does with Alex—but it's fairly obvious how she feels about him!' Harry grinned, putting his arm about Beth's waist and giving it a loving squeeze.

Lorna could feel a hot flush covering her face, and she was grateful for the opportunity to bend down and pat the head of a black labrador who had decided to join them. 'Has—has he known her long?' she asked carelessly. 'She—she's a very beautiful girl.'

'Absolutely stunning!' Harry agreed. 'She's the daughter of a rich industrial tycoon in Milan. Alex met her a couple of years ago when he went to take some photographs of the old boy and his new factory. She hasn't been to stay at the house before—to tell the truth, I was a bit surprised to see her. Alex never brings his birds down here, you see.'

'Why ever not?' Beth looked surprised, and Lorna found herself wishing that she hadn't asked for further details of the beautiful Italian girl. She seemed to be clutched firmly in the grip of raging jealousy, an emotion she had never experienced before and one that she had no idea how to combat. However, as she was fast discovering, rubbing salt in the wound was not the answer.

Harry led the way out of the courtyard, shrugging as he tried to answer Beth's question. 'Alex has got a thing about family being one matter, and what he calls, "passing birds of passage" being quite another. I remember him giving me some cousinly advice about girls—when I was much younger, of course!' He smiled broadly as Beth gave a hoot of derisive laughter.

'Anyway, that was when he told me that the only girl he'd ever have down here, was the one he wanted to marry. He may have a hell of a reputation—well, I know he has!—but Alex is surprisingly strict and old-fashioned underneath. What's more, he's always been jolly kind to Gussie and me,' he added gruffly.

'Where are we going?' Lorna asked, feeling that she had been listening to just about as much as she could stand.

'Ah . . . It's a surprise!' Harry grinned as he led them across the rich, spongy green grass of the park.

'Aren't you glad I bought you those boots, hmm?' Lorna murmured in her sister's ear.

'Damn right!' Beth laughed, kicking one leg up in the air. 'Now, if you'd been just as sensible yourself, you wouldn't be staggering around in an old pair of Harry's and—hey, watch out . . .!'

Lorna had unconsciously stepped on to what looked like a small brown patch on the grass, only finding out too late as the boot which was far too large for her feet skidded away beneath her, that cows used the park as well as sheep.

'Fancy forgetting to look out for cow-pats!' Beth teased. 'We've lived in New York too long, you know. Are you all right?' she asked anxiously, helping Lorna to her feet.

'Yes, I'm fine and I didn't get any of the filthy stuff on me, which is something, I suppose!'

'What are you two girls laughing about?' Harry who

had missed Lorna's fall, stopped and turned around to
see the sisters giggling helplessly together.

'Nothing, darling,' Beth gasped. 'Just—just admiring
the—er—mud!'

'You're both crazy. Still, it's been fun having you
here, Lorna. I wish you could stay longer with us.

'What—and play gooseberry to you two? No,
thanks!' she answered lightly, although she was touched
by Harry's words. Nevertheless, the fresh air was
helping to clear her head, and it was time she made
some definite plans to leave Oakeley Park just as soon
as she could.

They reached the other side of the wide green expanse
of wooded park, and walked down a small country lane
towards a large white five-bar gate. 'There, what do you
think of that?' Harry said, leaning on the gate and
looking at the house in front of them.

'It—it's lovely, Beth murmured, and Lorna agreed as
she looked at the long, low house, with heavy wooden
beams set in red brick under a pale gold thatched roof.

'That's good,' Harry laughed as he fished in his
pocket. 'Here you are, Mrs Kendall-to-be ... the keys
to your new home!'

'Oh—Harry ...!' Beth breathed ecstatically. 'Is it
really going to be ours ...? Oh—I—I can hardly believe
it! It's so lovely ...' She clutched his arm excitedly,
gazing up at him with stars in her eyes.

'We'd better wait until we see the inside of the place,
before you get too over the moon about it. Alex says that
it probably needs a lot doing to it,' Harry said, opening
the gate and issuing the girls through before him.

Lorna hesitated, looking at the house and then at the
young couple. 'No, I—I think I won't come in with
you,' she said slowly. 'Maybe tomorrow, if Beth wants
to look over it again, hmm?'

'Oh, Lorna!' Beth looked at her in disappointment.
'Don't you want to see my new house?'

'Of course I do, idiot! But—well, I think you and Harry ought to look over your future home on your own—for the first time anyway,' Lorna smiled gently at her sister.

'Oh, that's—that is understanding of you,' Beth murmured, giving her a breathless hug. 'Do you want to wait here, or . . .'

'No, I think I'll just take a nice, long walk back to the main house, OK? I'll see you later,' she called as she turned to walk back up the lane.

Moving slowly, her hands plunged deep in the pockets of the lightweight, cream-coloured raincoat belted tightly about her slim waist, Lorna hardly noticed where she was going. She was deeply ashamed of having felt a deep pang of envy, which had struck her so forcibly as she had watched her sister and Harry run excitedly towards their new home. What on earth had got into her? When she had come here to England, there had only been one object in her mind—to achieve her sister's happiness. Seeing Beth and Harry so content together, and knowing that they had the support of Alex and Gussie, should make her feel joyful, not low and depressed like this. There was no doubt that Mrs Kendall might prove to be a possible fly in the ointment, but as no one seemed to take her too seriously, it appeared to be only a slight cross Beth would have to bear.

She was in danger of becoming horribly selfish, she told herself sternly. Just because she hadn't expected their visit to turn out in the way it had—nor realised that in the process she would be losing not only her sister, but also her peace of mind . . . Well, that was just too bad, wasn't it? What she must do now was to think of a way she could leave this place as soon as possible.

But she couldn't. Trying to think calmly and logically seemed totally beyond her at the moment. Her whole mind was full of one thing and one thing only—her love for Alex. Why had she been so stupid as to fall in love with a man whose lifestyle made any chance of happiness with him so impossible? Not that he was interested in a future life together with her, anyway. But even if he was, their whole view on life was so totally different. Almost everywhere she looked, there seemed no point of similarity. She believed in fidelity in a relationship, while he didn't even know the meaning of the word! Despite what he'd said in the long gallery about wanting to settle down, she couldn't see him doing it—not when there were still beautiful women in the world. If he doesn't watch it, he'll become just like Jacques! she thought sourly.

All this was useless speculation, she realised. There could be no future for her with Alex, not when they only had one thing in common. Something she had instinctively known the moment she'd first laid eyes on him—the irresistible, powerful chains of an attraction that knew no reason. It had struck her down like a flash of lightning, and ever since she had been consumed by the raging flames of a fire which by now was quite out of control.

The rain was falling now in a heavy downpour. Her smart raincoat proved to be of little use in keeping out the wet which seeped in, soaking the polo-necked sweater and slacks she was wearing. Her hair fell in a long, bedraggled mess down her back, and for the first time in years, she didn't care what she looked like. It couldn't be worse than she felt, anyway.

The roar of an engine cut into her miserable thoughts, and she looked up to see a vehicle leave the long driveway and come bumping over the park towards her. Braking sharply, and skidding on the wet grass, a door was thrown open as in angry tones someone asked her what in the hell she thought she was doing?

Recognising the voice immediately, she raised a

shaking hand to brush the wet hair back from her face.
'I—I just felt like a walk . . .'

'In this weather? Are you crazy?' Alex shouted,
having to raise his voice above the loud patter of the
rain on the roof of the green Land Rover, and the
howling wind shaking a group of oak trees beside her.
'Jump in—and hurry up about it!' he commanded.

'No! I—I'm all right. I'll just keep on and . . .' She
got no further as he leapt out, quickly sweeping her slim
figure up in his arms and unceremoniously throwing her
into the vehicle. 'How—how dare you!' she gasped.
'Leave—leave me alone!'

'Cool it, lady!' Alex drawled. 'I did actually get the
message yesterday, you know. I certainly have no
intention of touching even a hair of your head, so why
don't you just relax, hmm?'

'Well, if you feel like that, why don't you let me get
out of this damned pick-up of yours?' she snarled, her
head almost bursting with frustrated longing to hit the
man sitting so calmly beside her.

'Because, *darling*, you're soaked through, and we
can't have you catching pneumonia, now can we?'

She suddenly felt sick, the hateful, sarcastic drawl in
his voice piercing her to the heart. 'Who are you
kidding? You couldn't care less!' she muttered angrily
before she realised just how childish she was being.
God! From the way she was behaving, anyone would
think she was still in the fourth grade at school . . .
Furious with herself, she turned away to look out of the
window, noticing that they were still stationary.

'Here,' Alex said, reaching behind him and draping a
rug around her shoulders. 'You look wet and miserable,
and I would indeed mind if you caught a cold—you
would undoubtedly pass it on to the rest of us!'

'Your charitable concern overwhelms me!' she
snapped, resting her head back on the seat and closing her
eyes as he started the engine and drove back to the house.

Alex had used the same drawling, sardonic tone to her last night, and at the end of the long, drawn-out meal she had felt like a worn-out dishrag. The last thing she'd wanted was to have to face everyone at dinner, and considering his upbringing you might have thought that he would have tried to act with some sophistication. But oh no! Not Alex Kendall!'

By the time she had finished making-up, trying to hide the ravages of her storm of tears in the bath, it was almost time to go downstairs for dinner. Telling Beth to go on down and she'd be along as soon as possible, she had hurriedly stepped into the long, warm cashmere dress which she had worn the night Alex had come back to the apartment in New York—the night he had first tried to make love to her. It must have stretched, or else she'd lost weight lately; either way, the deep V-shaped neck seemed somehow lower than usual and far too revealing. It had been too late for her to change, and she had hurried downstairs feeling sick and apprehensive about the evening which lay ahead.

As soon as she entered the drawing room, now in use with so many people staying in the house, she knew her dress was a mistake. Harry's joking wolf-whistle had alerted all eyes, and Jacques immediately started oozing his way towards her, his eyes riveted on her cleavage. Alex appeared at her side, handing her a drink and watching with cynical amusement as Lorna's nervous fingers nearly dropped the glass.

'Mmm—very nice, and very, very sexy,' he had drawled softly. 'So, just who are you going to tantalise tonight, I wonder? Poor old Jay isn't here, so it looks like my stepfather is the lucky chap! *Bon chance, mon brave!*' Alex laughed cruelly, slapping Jacques on the back before making his way over to murmur sweet nothings in Luci's ear.

Alex's bitter, taunting words left her feeling shattered, but even through her misery she had noted the Italian girl's dark-eyed, speculative gaze. There was no doubt as to the conclusions Luci had come to, baiting Lorna unmercifully throughout the meal. If she doesn't shut up, I'll throw my glass of wine in her face in a minute, Lorna had fumed as Luci continued her catty, joking references to the loose moral lives of those in the fashion business, and the crude, unsophisticated life led by Americans.

Surprisingly, it was Harry who leapt to her defence. 'Hey, just a moment,' he said, glaring into Luci's beautiful face. 'I'm going to marry one of your so-called "crude" Americans, and that's not how I see Beth at all! What's—what's more, I—I think Lorna's one of the nicest people I've ever met!'

'Bravo, Harry!' Lady Caroline clapped her hands. 'I, too, have been bored to sobs by this conversation for the last half hour. Now, tell me, Lorna,' she said, deliberately ignoring Luci, 'exactly where the French designers are going to put the waist this year?'

Which had been really very good of Lady Caroline, Lorna thought, especially since Jacques seemed to have four pairs of hands which Lorna had difficulty in keeping off her body . . .

'Wake up, sleeping beauty!' Alex shook her shoulder.

'I wasn't asleep,' she muttered, her teeth chattering at the draught from the open door of the vehicle now parked outside the front door of the house.

'You're frozen, you silly girl!' His voice grated harshly as he bent down, scooping her up in his arms. 'You'll feel much better after a hot bath.'

'I'm fine . . . really . . .' she breathed huskily, unable to prevent herself from relaxing against his broad shoulder. Her senses were bemused by the tanned skin of his cheek, only inches from her own face; her eyes drawn to the dark, damp hair curving over his collar and the tantalising, musky scent of his aftershave filled her nostrils. As he mounted the wide stone steps, she couldn't prevent a small sigh of contentment from escaping her lips, quickly lowering her eyelashes as he turned his head.

'Oh, Lorna!' he murmured. 'What on earth am I going to do with you, hmm?'

'You—you're going to put me down, please,' she muttered jerkily, still held firmly in his arms as he crossed the vast expanse of the hall; the unexpected warmth in his voice leaving her feeling weak and breathless.

'Not until I make sure that you are firmly upstairs, and you promise me to change out of these wet clothes. You, my dear girl, are soaking!'

She ought to at least put up some token of resistance, she told herself as he carried her swiftly up the marble staircase. But her body was shivering so uncontrollably from the damp cold clothes clinging to her skin, that she lay meekly in his arms until he kicked open the door of her bedroom.

'Right—off with those clothes!' he said sharply, letting go of her trembling figure.

'Yes, I—I will . . .' She hesitated as he stood looking at her with hard, stern eyes.

'Well, hurry up. What are you waiting for?'

'For you to leave my room, of course!' she snapped nervously.

'I wish I could believe that.' His mouth tightened into a hard line. 'Anyone who could be so stupid as to be out walking in that rain, and wearing a raincoat only suitable for strolling down Fifth Avenue, needs her head examined! I'm going to change myself, now, but I warn you, I'll be back in ten minutes, and if you haven't had a hot shower by then, I'll strip the clothes off you myself!'

She watched the door bang behind his angry figure, before turning wearily to peel off the soaking layers of wet cloth and going through to stand under the shower.

He was right, of course, but there was no need for him to have been so horrid to her. All that famous charm seemed to have disappeared overnight, certainly as far as she was concerned, anyway.

Having shampooed her hair as well, she slipped into a warm white towelling robe before going to sit down in front of her dressing table to blow-dry the long golden stream of hair. Alex's anger was understandable in the context of her rejection of him yesterday, but ... she paused, the thought suddenly coming into her mind that she was surprised he could be so petty. Despite the cruel words she had used to him, she couldn't have been the only woman to have said 'no', although there probably hadn't been many. Surely such an experienced man would just laugh and shrug off the disappointment—busily moving off to fresh fields and pastures new? Maybe she didn't really know him at all, but she could have sworn that he was behaving very oddly, quite out of character in fact.

Lorna rested the hairdryer in her lap for a moment while she thought about how kind Alex had been to Beth, smoothing her path towards marrying Harry, and laying down the law to Mrs Kendall. And she didn't suppose there had been any outside pressure forcing him to be so kind to his cousins, either, looking after their welfare since they were small and still keeping a fatherly eye on them. She sighed deeply, drifting off into a happy, hopelessly romantic daydream which she knew had no foundation in real life, when she was startled by a knock on the door. Oh Lord! He'd said he'd be coming back, and ...

'Ah, I see you have been sensible, after all—wonders will never cease!'

She could feel her face burning at the cruelly sardonic expression in his voice. She had become so sensitive to his barbed tongue in the last two days, that she didn't seem to have any fight left in her.

'I ... I ... er ... you were quite right. I feel much better. I don't know why I got so wet, I ...' She could hear herself gabbling away nervously and there didn't seem to be a damn thing she could do about it. Just looking at him made her feel weak as she desperately tried to stop her knees from knocking nervously together. She gazed in the mirror at the long length of his legs in the slim-fitting, dark grey slacks, the black cashmere sweater which emphasised his tan and clung to his broad shoulders, and tried to control herself as she trembled with an insane desire to leap up and run into his arms.

She saw him frown at her incoherent chatter and walk slowly over to stand looking down at her. 'Are you feeling all right?' His voice seemed to come from some way off as he placed a warm hand on her forehead. 'It feels cool enough,' he murmured, his eyes turning to gaze at her reflection in the mirror.

What does he see? she wondered, almost flinching at the sight of her tousled and disordered hair, the full swollen lips parting breathlessly as his hand gently lifted a gold coil from the mass of newly washed hair cascading down her back. She shivered almost uncontrollably as his fingers moved to stroke the smooth skin of her neck. She was unable to move, unable to speak or tear her eyes away from his in the still silence of the room, his hand slipping down inside her robe to slowly caress the swollen fullness of her breasts, the rosy tips taut and aching for his touch.

'Alex, please!' Was that hoarse, panic-stricken voice really hers? She gasped, a low, husky moan breaking from her throat as he pulled aside her robe, both hands now caressing her breasts, the glittering blue eyes still firmly locked with hers in the mirror.

'Oh God ... *Lorna!*' The harsh cry broke from his lips as he jerked her to her feet, spinning her around and ruthlessly crushing her in his arms as he stared down intently for a moment into the slanting green eyes glazing with desire. A raging fever seemed to possess her, her senses blind to everything as her mouth parted, thirsting for his kiss.

She could feel herself being swept along on a wave of pure pleasure, her whole world encompassed by the strength of his arms and the pressure of his mouth on hers. Mindless with passionate desire she frantically arched her body against him, her small moans of pleasure provoking a deep groan in his throat. Suddenly he lifted his head, putting a warning hand over her mouth as her lips opened to protest at his abrupt withdrawal.

'Shush . . .!' he bent forward to whisper in her ear, and it was only some seconds later that she heard Beth and Harry coming along the corridor, laughing and joking together.

'Are you all right, Lorna?' Beth called out. 'We got absolutely soaked and so we'll change and see you later at tea, OK?'

'Yes . . . I'm fine . . .' she managed to croak, standing within Alex's arms and listening as the engaged couple gave each other an enthusiastic kiss, before Harry strode off whistling down the corridor. Alex must have the hearing of a cat, she thought, or maybe he really was the dangerous panther-like animal she had recognised back in New York.

'I'm sorry,' he murmured, giving her a swift kiss on the forehead. 'I didn't mean to startle you.' He gently drew the sides of her robe together. 'But I knew you wouldn't want your sister to see you like this.' His words broke the spell she had been under, and she blushed with shame at having so easily fallen victim to his overwhelming attraction once more.

'You're suddenly very conscious of the proprieties— I'm impressed!' she hissed angrily. 'Or was it to make sure that Beth didn't have anything to tell Luci, hmm?'

Lorna nearly cried out as a firm hand brutally grasped her chin, forcing her head up to meet his glittering blue eyes, the murderous rage she saw in their depths making her feel suddenly frightened.

'What in the bloody hell has Luci to do with my kissing you?' His menacing voice was soft and dangerous.

'You . . . you might well ask? Kissing me while you've been busy romancing her as well as myself—only apparently you're going to marry her, the poor fool! God, you really are the living end!'

In some way that she didn't even begin to understand, Lorna was actually gaining a perverse pleasure from hitting back at Alex. Her tortured emotions were crying out for vengence and she was past caring what she said or did.

'Well, run along then,' she managed to smile into the harsh contours of his strained face. 'You've just got time for a quick lovemaking session with the glamorous Lucrezia Borgia, before you grab a reviving cup of tea and come racing back to see me again! You've certainly got stamina—I'll say that for you—or don't you believe in making love to the girl you're going to marry? What delicacy . . .' she added recklessly. 'What finesse! Who would have guessed that the randy Lord Alex—Ah . . .!'

Lorna put a trembling hand to her stinging cheek, her eyes glazed with shock. 'You—you slapped me . . .'

'I've never—*ever*—hit a woman in my life, but by God you've been asking for that for a long time!' She could never have believed that Alex could be so angry, his figure shaking almost uncontrollably as he fought to master his fury.

'What is it with you, lady?' he demanded roughly, when he could find his voice. 'Ever since I've known you, you've done nothing but spit and claw at me like some hell-cat. And I, to my shame, have kept persevering in what I now see was a vain hope—that one day you could learn to love me. More fool I!' he laughed harshly, pushing his hands roughly through his dark hair.

'My God—it's ironic, isn't it? The only girl I've ever truly loved—the only one I've ever wanted to marry—turns out to be a raving nut case! I've never known anything like it! You melt lovingly into my arms one moment and insult me the next—*Jesus!* you've really put me through it, haven't you, Lorna?'

'Alex . . .! I . . .' It was if she was suddenly standing on a tiny piece of ground and all about her there was a void. She could hardly comprehend what he was saying, and yet she wanted to cry out with pain as his words jabbed like a dagger in her heart. 'Please, Alex . . .' she put out a trembling hand towards him.

'Why don't you do us both a favour, hmm? Why don't you go back to your nice, safe apartment in New York? You'll be all right there. You can lock yourself away in your ivory tower—or marry Jay Holden—and never have to deal with real people or real emotions!'

'That's not true! I—I'm not like that!' she cried.

Alex's shoulders slumped as he ignored her words and walked slowly towards the door. 'I've taken all I'm prepared to take from you, Lorna. Maybe I would be better off marrying Luci, after all. I'd know where I stood with her, which is more that I've ever known with you. At least she doesn't treat me as if I was the devil incarnate!' he added bitterly.

'Alex . . .' she moaned.

'Forget it, Lorna,' he said wearily. 'I simply don't care any more . . .' his voice trailed away as he quietly closed the door behind him.

Lorna had no clear recollection of what she did during the next hour. She was shaking so hard that she found it difficult to co-ordinate her limbs, even staggering over to collapse on her bed had taken all her strength. If she thought that she had ever suffered pain before, she now knew how mistaken she had been. Her

whole mind and body was a throbbing mass of misery,
her brain frozen and incapable of any thought as
nausea welled up inside her and she rushed into the
bathroom.

An hour later, Lorna looked numbly around the
room to see if she had forgotten anything. She had no
idea what she had packed into her small overnight case,
and quite honestly she didn't care. The only certainty in
her whole existence was the knowledge that she must
leave immediately, if for no other reason than Alex had
told her to.

She couldn't even bear to think about him, the pain
was too great and it only brought on the bitter spasms
that had kept her running to be sick in the bathroom
during the last hour. She had managed to struggle into
an old pair of jeans and a warm jumper, but still her
body shivered with nervous tension, her hands shaking
as if she had the palsy.

Where she would go for the night she had no idea.
There must be some hotel in London which could put
her up, she supposed dully. But—but she must write a
short note for Beth. Maybe if she said that she had
been suddenly called away to do a job . . .? Yes, that
was what she would say. Looking about her distractedly for a pen, she realised that it was in her
handbag. Handbag . . .? Oh, no! It was downstairs in
the back hall where she'd left it when she had
changed to go out for the walk with Harry and Beth
this afternoon. She'd have to go and get it, if only
because it held all her money and passport. But how?
If she went down the main staircase, she might—she
might bump into Alex . . . The thought frightened her
so much, that she had to sit down to catch her
breath. But maybe if she went down the back
staircase she'd be safe? She decided that she must
take the risk.

Walking as quietly as she could down the corridor,

Lorna passed the open door of a bedroom almost before she realised that she had done so.

'Come in, darling, and let me see what you've decided to wear tonight,' Lady Caroline's voice rang out.

Slowly and hesitantly retracing her steps, Lorna hovered unhappily in the doorway.

'Oh, I see you haven't changed yet,' Alex's mother looked at Lorna's jeans with a smile, her expression changing as she raised her eyes and saw the naked misery on the girl's face. 'Darling!' she cried, jumping to her feet and going swiftly over to the door. 'Whatever is it?'

'I . . .' Lorna tried to clear her throat, but she found she couldn't speak.

'Come along, darling. Come with me,' Lady Caroline murmured softly, putting an arm around Lorna's shoulders and gently leading her into the large, softly lit bedroom. 'Now, you just sit down there, hmm?' she said, drawing up a comfortable chair, 'and there's no need to worry. Dear Jacques has already changed and gone downstairs, so we're quite alone.'

Lorna suddenly felt more tired than she could ever remember. Lady Caroline's voice was soft and soothing, and she could feel the rigor mortis which had seemed to be affecting her limbs, causing them to be stiff and jerky, slowly dying away.

'Now, darling, you tell me all about it. I can see that something is terribly wrong.'

The thought of even begining to try and tell Alex's mother about all that had happened, made Lorna tremble violently. 'I'm—I'm sorry . . . You're being very—kind, I . . .' She shook her head distractedly, and tried to force herself to rise from the chair.

'Now calm down, Lorna.' Lady Caroline's authoritative voice broke through the miasma of her thoughts, and she subsided wearily back into the chair. 'It is obvious that you're in trouble of some kind. Is it your sister?'

'No, I . . . No, she's fine.'

'Well, that's a relief! Sophie can be an absolute bitch sometimes, and I've already taken the liberty of telling her that one unkind word to your sister, and she is strictly out—O.U.T.'

'That's so very kind of you,' Lorna murmured gratefully. 'Beth loves Harry very much, and—and I know they'll be—they'll be very h-happy . . .' To her absolute horror she found herself crying, and not silent tears, but wrenching, tearing sobs that violently shook her body.

'That's right, darling, you let it all come out—you'll feel so much better for it, believe me.' The older woman got up and pressed some tissues into Lorna's hand. 'Now,' she added, as the tears slowly died away, 'if it isn't your sister, then I can only assume that it is Alex who is causing you to be so unhappy, hmm?'

Lorna, her face buried in the tissues, could only nod. 'I might have known that my stupid son would bungle matters,' his mother sighed. 'Darling, he's so terribly in love with you, that he can't even see straight any more.'

'No, he's n-not,' Lorna sobbed. 'He—he doesn't want to s-see me ever again . . .' her words finishing in a heart-breaking wail.

'Stuff and nonsense!' Lady Caroline laughed.

'No—you don't understand. It—it's all my fault. I—I simply didn't dare to t-take him seriously, you see. His—well, his reputation . . .' she found she couldn't continue. How could she possibly tell Alex's mother about that?

The older woman laughed again. 'Don't try and spare my feelings, my dear girl! Darling Alex had been a *very* naughty boy in the past, I'm afraid. But he's certainly a reformed character now, and very serious about you. After all, darling, that's why I'm here, isn't it?'

Lorna looked at her in shock. 'Why you're here?' she repeated in complete confusion.

'Of course. I was a little fed up with him, until he explained. I mean, dear Jacques and I were all set to go to stay with some friends in Cannes for Easter. But when he told me that he wanted me to meet the girl he hoped to marry—well, I came over like a shot, darling! Surely you knew that's why we're here?'

Lorna blew her nose and sighed wearily. 'It seems I was the last to know anything—even that he loved me! It's a bit of a laugh, isn't it?' she added bitterly. 'Never mind, you'll find, when you talk to your *dear* son, that he's now decided to change his arrangements, somewhat. Just stick around and you'll undoubtedly be invited to his wedding—to Luci!'

CHAPTER NINE

'His what?' Lady Caroline threw back her dark head and roared with laughter. 'Alex is never going to marry that hot little number—not in a million years! Darling, Lorna, what a surprisingly innocent girl you are. Didn't you know that Luci's reputation is notorious—my dear, she's had more men than I've had hot dinners! And while I must admit that she's outstandingly beautiful, she's hardly what my son would regard as wife and mother material, now is she?'

'He said he was thinking of marrying her,' Lorna muttered, staring down at her nervously twisting hands.

'If you've turned him down flat, he may well have said something like that in the heat of the moment, but I'd stake my life that he's not seriously intending to do anything of the sort!' Alex's mother paused for a moment, looking at the girl's bent head and hunched figure before turning away to pick up a hairbrush from the dressing table. 'Did you ... did you turn him down?' she asked casually.

'If—if you asking whether he proposed marriage to me—the answer is that no, he didn't. I'm not even sure that he said he loved me ...' Lorna pushed a weary hand across her forehead. 'We had such a row, you see, and it was mostly my fault. I was ... I said some stupid things about Luci, and ...' she shrugged helplessly. 'Anyway, he told me to leave this place, and that's it, really.'

Lady Caroline sat staring at Lorna for some time, slowly revolving the hairbrush in her hand. 'So, you're just going to run away, are you?' she said. 'That's odd, because you didn't strike me as the type, somehow.'

'Type ...' What type?' Lorna looked at her in confusion.

'Oh, you know ...' the older woman waved a hand dismissively and changed the subject. 'It's funny, but we've hardly had any opportunity to talk together, you and I. What made you decide to be a fashion model?'

What on earth was she doing, sitting here in this room and being expected to calmly discuss her career with Alex Kendall's mother? The whole situation seemed totally bizarre, to say the least. Still, the older woman had been kind and sympathetic ... 'Money,' she answered, grimacing with wry amusement at the surprised look on Lady Caroline's face.

'My father, who I had always thought of as a wealthy man, died heavily in debt, and my sister was just finishing school with a promising musical career ahead of her. The only assets I had were a wardrobe of good clothes, some decent jewellery, a large apartment in Manhattan and a strong constitution. In fact, being fit and healthy proved to be the most important attribute I possessed,' she added ruefully. 'If a girl wants to be a model, unless she's as strong as a horse, she won't be able to stand the pace. During the Paris collections, for instance, I get up at six in the morning, and I'm seldom in bed before midnight—and I've been working solidly all the time. The life is a killer!'

'Darling—this is fascinating! Do go on.'

'I can't think why you're interested,' Lorna shrugged. 'I had been to drama school, so I knew how to act, but I couldn't earn enough in the theatre to support my sister and myself, not immediately. The same criteria applied to films, of course. And then I had an idea. What else does a model do, but act out for the general public the idea behind a designer's clothes? I was tall and thin and I reckoned I could do it. So, I went to Henri Bendel's, where I'd been a client in the past, and persuaded them to give me a chance as a house model. As it turned out, I happened to have the right face and the right figure for the style that year. I learnt the ropes there, and then branched out as a freelance—and that's it, really.'

'And you managed to make enough money to keep yourself and your sister?' Lady Caroline probed.

Lorna shrugged. 'It depends on what you call "enough". On just modelling alone last year, I made over one hundred and fifty thousand dollars. Together with the income from my savings, and various endorsements like face powder, TV ads, etc., I guess I pull in half a million dollars per year, one way and another.'

'My goodness! Well done!' Alex's mother smiled gently. 'I wasn't asking you about your past just from idle curiosity, Lorna. I wanted to know what sort of girl you are, and it's obvious that you have guts and determination. Equally obvious is the fact that the fashion world is hardly a bed of roses, and to survive as a top model you must have a lot of spunk. Something, if you don't mind me saying so, you seem to be lacking at the moment!' She smiled, the curve of her lips, so like that of her son's, taking the sting from her words. 'My darling girl, if you could stand up and fight for what you wanted once—then surely you could do so again, hmm?'

'I only wish it was as easy as that,' Lorna shrugged unhappily. 'I'm not running away from Alex just because he told me to go,' she added. 'I'm leaving because there is simply no point in my staying here for one minute longer. In fact, I should never have come in the first place, except that I promised my sister I would. The last person I expected to see was Alex, and as for him telling you that he wanted to marry me—I'm afraid I find it difficult to believe ...' She paused and sighed, running nervous, trembling fingers through her long gold hair. 'I'm sorry to have been so silly—crying and making a fool of myself just now. God! I'm twenty-five and should know better, I really should . . .'

'Darling, we're all hopeless when it comes to matters of the heart!'

'Yes, that's been the trouble all along with Alex and myself. I—well, it took me a very long time to admit that I was in love with him, and even then it all seemed so hopeless—and still does. I really don't want to be rude, especially as you're his mother, but his reputation stinks—as far as I'm concerned, anyway. I thought that he just wanted to add me to his list of conquests, and I want and need far more from a man that than. I'm still not convinced . . .' Lorna shrugged. 'I'm sorry, that's how it is.'

'But darling, you can't have expected him to have been a monk all these years, now can you?'

'No, of course not. But I can hardly be expected to believe that he's suddenly become whiter than white, either.'

'Oh, Lorna.' The older woman looked at her sadly. 'There is nothing safe or certain in this world, you must know that. We all have, at one time or another, to hold our nose and dive blindly into life. Two people have to learn to trust one another. What is a loving relationship without trust, hmm?'

'But that—that's what I mean! How can I possibly trust Alex to suddenly turn over a new leaf? How do I know that he won't be sneaking off, first chance he can get, to romance some gorgeous woman? And—and it would break my heart if he did,' she sniffed, her eyes filling with tears again.

'Well, I trust Jacques. I know,' Lady Caroline laughed, 'he's an outrageous flirt—and why not? He's getting on now, of course, but when he was younger, he was absolutely lethal! Women flung themselves at him right, left and centre, and I don't mind admitting that I got pretty fed up at times. But the point is: he married me, when I was honestly a bit past my prime, and has never tried to cheat on me once. Why should he, when I strive to make him happy?'

'Yes, well . . . you haven't got to watch Luci climbing all over him, not like she is over Alex!' Lorna said grimly.

'Honestly, darling, I think your wits must be addled. It was *Jacques* who brought her down here—a ghastly mistake, I freely admit. Alex didn't invite her, did he?'

'Well, she's here now—and to stay from the look of things,' Lorna sighed wearily, getting up from her chair. 'I—I must go. I can't thank you enough for being so very kind and trying to help me calm down. I'm—well, I'm really very sorry that you aren't going to be my mother-in-law after all,' she smiled weakly.

'I'm sorry too, you beautiful, but hopelessly stubborn girl. May God preserve me from the trauma of star-crossed lovers!' Lady Caroline groaned impatiently. 'What are you going to do now?'

'I have to write a letter to Beth—I thought I'd say something about a job having come up. But I've left my pen downstairs in my bag. I was on my way to get it just now. I—er—I didn't want to go down the front staircase, just in case . . .'

'You didn't want to meet Alex—very understandable Then what? Driving yourself to London? Here, take my pen,' she said as Lorna nodded. 'I'll go down and get your bag for you while you write your letter to your sister. I'm in no hurry, since I haven't decided what to wear for this boring dinner party we've all been invited to, anyway.'

Lorna looked at Lady Caroline. 'I was thinking yesterday that with your colouring, you ought to wear scarlet—it would look magnificent with your tan and dark hair.'

'Oh what a pity it is that you insist on taking yourself

out of my life! We could have been *such* good friends, you and I.' She sighed. 'Ah, well . . . Now take the pen, and I'll be up with your bag in a moment.'

'There's really no need . . .'

'Lorna—I'll shake you in a moment! Stop being tiresome, and just do as I say, darling, hmm?'

With a slight smile, Lorna shrugged and with the pen in her hand walked slowly back to her room.

It was half an hour later before Lady Caroline arrived back with her bag. 'I'm sorry, darling, to have been so long, but one of the servants had tidied it away. Incidentally, I've had a simply marvellous idea! You know we're all supposed to be going out to this dinner party? Well, how about if I say that I've seen you and that you've got a really sick headache, far too ill to come with us. If you wait until everyone has gone—you can easily hear the cars driving away from up here in this room—then you can go down and out to the garage without having to bump into anyone!'

Lady Caroline seemed almost as eager to get rid of her as her son, Lorna thought gloomily, and then felt ashamed of being so ungrateful for all the other woman's help. 'Yes, that seems a good idea . . .' she agreed listlessly.

'Splendid! Where are you going to stay when you get to London?' Lady Caroline asked.

Lorna shrugged. 'I—I don't quite know. Maybe I can find a hotel . . .'

'Oh, yes, you're easily bound to find somewhere. Well, goodbye, Lorna, take care of yourself, won't you?' Alex's mother gave her a cheerful kiss, and walked humming from the room.

I thought she liked me, but maybe she's changed her mind about Luci, Lorna told herself, sinking into deep depression. Now it had actually come to the point, she was finding it hard to leave, even though she knew that Alex wanted her to go. Propping up the letter to Beth on her dressing table, she went over to open the window to make sure of hearing when everyone left the house.

It seemed an age before the members of the household managed to organise their departure. Listening to the distant murmur of talk and laughter, Lorna felt ineffably lonely and miserable. Despite all that had happened during her short stay in the huge house, she knew that she would miss the timeless atmosphere of its old stone walls and large, comfortable rooms, the woodsmoke from the huge fireplaces with the dogs snoring in front of them, and the tranquil peace of the lush green acres stretching away as far as the eye could see.

She had to stop thinking like that, she told herself roughly, forcing her lethargic, tired body away from the window and over to the bed where her packed case was waiting. Taking one last look around the room, she slipped into the warm comfort of her grey fox coat before walking slowly out through the door and on down the corridor.

She had just reached the bottom step of the wide marble staircase, and was trying to remember just which door led to the courtyard containing the garage, when she heard a step in the hall.

'Ah, there you are, Lorna. You've certainly been taking your time.'

'*Alex . . .!*' she gasped, almost fainting with shock and desperately clutching at the banister rail of the staircase for support.

'Come on, give me your suitcase.'

'W-what . . .? I . . . What are you d-doing here . . .?' Through dazed eyes she looked at his tanned, inscrutable face, devoid of all expression. Even his eyes were hard and enigmatic as he leant casually against a marble pillar.

'Well, I might remind you, yet again, that this is my house,' he drawled quietly. 'However, my mother said she felt you were in no fit state to drive to London tonight, and I agree with her. You look dreadful.'

'Your mother . . .? How could she do this to me?' Lorna wailed, almost crying with frustration and rage at what she could only see as a gross betrayal.

'You are a guest in our house. As my mother pointed out, how could we possibly let you go in the state you're obviously in? You'd probably smash yourself up on the first bend in the road.'

His curt, hard tones made her tremble. 'You—you can't keep me here!' she cried, looking wildly about her.

'Oh, for God's sake!' Alex groaned with impatience. 'I stayed behind with the express purpose of driving you to London, myself. At least we'll get you there in one piece and not in a hearse,' he added brutally.

'You—you're really making sure of getting rid of me!' she retorted, ashamed at not being able to control the unhappy wobble in her voice.

'Precisely!'

Lorna was too shaken by his sudden appearance and so thoroughly miserable at his indecent haste in wanting to get rid of her, that she listlessly allowed him to take the case from her trembling hand. It was only when he led the way to the front door that she began to pull herself together.

'This isn't the way to the garage.'

'No, we're going in my car,' he threw the words curtly over his shoulder.

'But I have a car in the garage, and—and it's hired. I must take it back . . .'

'You can leave it for Beth or Aunt Sophie's chauffeur can drive it up to London later. Come on, hurry up.'

Lorna seethed with rage. But there was nothing she could do, was there? The sooner she got to London the better, and if it meant having to go in this hateful man's car, so be it. She decided to ignore the small voice of reason that pointed out the justice of Lady Caroline's concern. She probably wasn't in a fit state to drive, but there had been absolutely no need for him to be so damned rude and insulting. Even if she did look dreadful—whose fault was it anyway?

'My God, what's that?' Lorna gazed at the long, low gunmetal-grey car, unlike anything she had ever seen before. 'You sure do have some weird automobiles,' she sniffed dismissively. 'What are we going to have to do— pedal our way up to London?'

Alex gave a dry bark of laughter. 'It is a Bristol Brigand Turbo, and handmade here in Britain. I can assure you that it goes very fast indeed, with remarkably little pedal power!' he said, opening the passenger door and throwing her case on to the back seat.

'So, you've got a fast car—big deal!' she snapped, stalking past him and easing herself into the deep leather seat. He closed her door, which shut with a quiet click, and walked around to join her.

'Fasten your seatbelt, please,' he instructed curtly.

'I would, if I could fix the damn thing,' she muttered nervously. Her heart thumped at the touch of his fingers brushing lightly over her breasts as he adjusted the tangled belt.

'All set?'

'As if I had a choice!' she muttered, sinking down into the comfortable, yielding, soft leather seat, and praying that the car was as fast as he had said. The sooner she got away from his stern, angry dark figure, the better!

They had been travelling for some time before Lorna accepted the inevitable: she simply wasn't going to be able to sleep She had closed her eyes immediately they had left Oakeley Park, desperately hoping that she could manage to complete the journey in an unconscious state. But that comfort insisted on eluding her, despite or because of her utter exhaustion.

Alex had remained totally silent so far, guiding the car through the country lanes with consummate skill. They were passing through a small town before joining the motorway, and in the light from the street lamps she could see his long tanned fingers resting firmly on the driving wheel, the stiff cuff of his white evening shirt gleaming palely against the black velvet jacket. Stealing a secret glance through her eyelashes at his stern profile, the lines and planes of his features looking strained in the flickering light, Lorna clasped her hands tightly together. She must ... she simply *must* learn to control and master this sick urge to press herself up against his strong shoulders, the impulse to brush away the stray lock of hair falling from his brow ... A small moan involuntarily escaped her lips, and she quickly turned it into a cough.

'Are you all right, Lorna?' He turned his head to glance quickly at the woman who had been sitting so silently beside him. 'Would you like me to switch on some music?'

She averted her head to stare out at the inky darkness, thankful that it was night and he couldn't see the hectic flush which had covered her face at the warm concern in his voice. He hadn't meant it, he was just being polite, she told herself fiercely as she tried to control her rapid breathing.

'Yes, I—I'm all right, and—and some music would be fine.'

Some moments later she realised her mistake, as the haunting strains of 'Bailero' from the *Songs of the Auvergne* filled the car. The singer's voice had a raw edge that tugged unmercifully at Lorna's tortured heart, her eyes filling with tears that overflowed to slide in a steady stream down her cheeks. She didn't dare reach into her bag for a handkerchief, since it might alert Alex to her distress, and she simply couldn't bear to contemplate the glint of sardonic amusement she knew she would see in his eyes.

How long she had lain back in her seat, her eyes tightly gripped together to try and control her weeping, she had no idea. It was only when she felt her seat belt being released that she realised they had arrived. But where? Through the shimmering prisms of the tear drops trembling on her lashes, she saw that Alex had stopped the car in a quiet London street of Georgian houses.

'Where—where are we?' she whispered, trying to keep her head averted from his gaze as her fingers reached down, searching for her handbag. 'I—I haven't thought about—about what hotel . . .'

Ignoring her words, he came around to open the passenger door, helping her to alight and swearing angrily under his breath as he saw her tear-stained face illuminated by the street lights. 'You stupid girl,' he growled, taking out his handkerchief and gently wiping her eyes. She was far too emotionally exhausted to protest, either then or when he led her faltering feet up some steps and removed a key chain from his pocket to open the front door of a large house.

It was only when they entered the elegant hall that she realised she was not in a hotel at all. 'Where are we?' she asked, looking about her in confusion.

'We are in my house. And I don't want any arguments from you, Lorna. It is quite clear that you are not in a fit state to go anywhere tonight, and certainly not to a hotel. It's all right,' he added bitterly as she flinched at his words, 'I'm not intending to lay a finger on you—so relax, hmm? Come on, I'll show you up to a bedroom, and I suggest that you have a long, hot bath.'

'Because I look "dreadful" I suppose!' she hissed, anger coming to her aid as she followed him up the stairs.

Alex gave a dry laugh. 'Vanity—thy name is woman! Tell a woman that she's looking beautiful, and she doesn't believe you. Tell her she looks dreadful, and her whole day is smashed to smithereens.'

'Well, you're the expert on women!' she muttered as he opened a door and issued her into a large bedroom.

'Absolutely right, Lorna, I am! And isn't that lucky, since I know that what you want at this moment is a strong drink and a hot bath—all of which I am going to provide, if you will just take that scowl off your face!' He walked over to a door on the other side of the room. Here's the bathroom. There should be plenty of bath oil, and I think you will find that the towels are warm. In here,' he opened a cupboard, 'you will find whisky, gin and brandy. Shall I pour you a drink now?'

Lorna leaned weakly aginst the wall and sighed deeply. There was absolutely no point in protesting any more. He was right, she did want a drink and a bath. Considering everything, Alex was being really kind ... Yes, please, I'd like a brandy,' she murmured, closing her eyes in tiredness for a moment before she felt him place the glass in her hand.

'Now, relax, hmm?' he murmured, running a tanned finger down her tear-stained cheek. 'Go and have your bath, and I'll organise something to eat.'

'Yes, I—I am grateful, Alex,' she stuttered, staring fixedly at his black, evening bow tie. 'I—er—I'm sorry to have been such a ...'

'... Confounded nuisance? Difficult problem ...? Profound enigma ...? Yes, Lorna, you've certainly been all those!' he laughed. She looked up, startled by the different tone in his voice, but his lids masked all expression in his eyes. 'I'll see you later,' he added as he walked over to the door.

Lorna lay in the large bath, her mind a complete blank. She was only aware that the strain and tension of the day was being soothed away by the soft oil and warm water, and that for the moment she simply wasn't capable of any logical thought process. Very slowly

and gradually, she came back to life, and looked sleepil
around the room. It was a very masculine bathroom, sh
realised, the short, dark blue towelling robe on the back o
the door, for instance, was surely a man's? A fe\
moments later, she realised from the shaving equipmen
by the basin, and from the musky, male scent of the bath
oil being released by the warmth of the water, that thi
was Alex's bathroom. And, therefore, it logicall
followed that the room next door must be his, too
Which—which meant that he had given her his room.

She lay and considered this deduction for a while
without coming to any real conclusion, except that h
was being unexpectedly kind. A knock at the doo
interrupted her confused thoughts.

'I hope you haven't gone to sleep in there,' Alex'
faintly amused tones called out. 'If you feel like comin\
downstairs, I'll fix you some scrambled eggs on toast—
they're the only thing I know how to cook!'

Stepping out of the bath and wrapping herself in a
towel, she cautiously opened and put her head aroun\
the door. Relieved to see that the room was empty
Lorna went over to her case, frowning with annoyanc
when she saw that she had forgotten to pack her robe
which she must have left at Oakeley Park. She went bacl
into the bathroom and lifted down Alex's towelling robe
which while it was short, was far too large. With a shru\
she reminded herself that beggars can't be choosers, an\
knotting the belt tightly about her waist, she left the roon
to make her way downstairs.

Wandering through the strange house, her bare fee
trod silently on the thick carpet as she unexpectedl\
came upon Alex, his long figure lying stretched out on a
dark red leather couch. Unaware of her presence, he la\
with his eyes closed, his face looking so tired and strained
that Lorna was suddenly swept by an overwhelming tid\
of aching, compassionate love. She gave a slight sigh
the sound alerting him to her appearance as his eye

napped open, narrowing thoughtfully as he viewed the unguarded expression on her face.

Her mouth was dry with fear and tension as she stood, incapable of movement, while he rose from the couch and walked slowly towards her. Alex had discarded his velvet dinner jacket and tie, and was wearing only the silk evening shirt and dark trousers. The strong, tanned column of his throat rose from the unbuttoned neck of his shirt, which was stretched tightly over his broad shoulders, the trousers cut to emphasise his narrow waist and tapering hips. Lorna couldn't move, standing paralysed as he came to a halt only a few inches from her trembling figure, her gaze trapped by the blue eyes staring down so intently into hers.

'Well, Lorna . . .?' he murmured, making no attempt to touch her. She flicked a nervous tongue over her dry lips, her heart pounding loudly and her breath quickening as the silence in the still room seemed to pound in her head.

'Do you want some supper?' he asked softly. She shook her head, managing to tear her eyes away from his at last and staring blindly down at the floor. 'So what is it that you do want, hmm?'

She couldn't for the life of her reply to his quiet question as a warm hand gently tilted her chin upwards, her body quivering and shaking almost uncontrollably in answer to the unmistakable, darkening gleam in his eyes.

'My darling . . . You must know that I love you with all my heart,' he whispered softly, his hands slowly moving forward to close on her hips. 'I want to marry you, and live happily with you for the rest of my days.' He paused, his eyes carefully searching her face as he gradually drew her closer to him. 'Oh, God! Please believe me, darling . . .' he breathed, lowering his head to bury his face in her hair.

All the pent-up emotions Lorna had been suppressing for so long, escaped in a long, shuddering sigh.

Moaning huskily, she wound her slim arms up around his neck as she lay quietly at peace against his body, hearing the muffled beating of his heart and realising, at last, that for her the fight was over. Nothing seemed to matter, neither the unhappy past nor the uncertain future. The only reality lay in the present as Alex pulled her body possessively into his tight embrace, a triumphant exclamation of joy breaking from his throat at her surrender. The next moment she found herself swept up in his arms and carried swiftly back up the stairs, not even the crash as Alex kicked open the bedroom door breaking into her trance-like haze of peace and happiness.

Setting her gently on the large bed, he bent to kiss the lips parting breathlessly and eagerly beneath his. Her body seemed to burn with a tormenting urgency as his mouth moved heatedly on her own, relishing the strength and leashed force of the arms tightening in an unbreakable circle about her slim figure. He gave a soft groan as his lips left hers to trace a lingering path down the long line of her throat. As if savouring every moment, his hands moved to untie her belt and slowly open her robe, his eyes darkening as he gently pushed aside the towelling fabric to reveal the fine bones and soft skin of her bare shoulders, the burgeoning fullness of her breasts.

'Lorna ...! My God, how I love you—from the very first moment I saw you!' he breathed unsteadily. She felt a fierce tide of excitement flow through her body at his words, her pulses racing at the dark flush beneath his tan as his eyes devoured her body. And then he was swiftly stripping off his clothes, her eyes widening in appreciation of his hard masculine body as he removed and tossed away her robe, before clasping her tightly in his arms.

'So lovely ...' he whispered, his hands moving softly over her waist and up to slowly caress her breasts, bending his dark head to kiss first one swollen peak and then another. Lorna gasped, moaning incoherently with

mindless pleasure as his tongue erotically stroked her soft
skin, her mind reeling almost out of control with
rapturous excitement at the mastery of his touch. This
was what her body had craved since their first meeting,
the response demanded by the powerful force of her
senses, driving her unerringly towards her destiny.

Tremors of delight now shivered across her skin,
shafts of exquisite pain exploding deep in her stomach
as he trailed his mouth downwards, tenderly caressing
and savouring the arousal of her flesh. And then his
touch became more insistent, his breathing ragged and
uneven in response to her movements, as lost in time
and space she writhed eagerly and sensually beneath
him, seeking the satisfaction that only he could
give. Pausing for a moment as if to imprint on his brain
the sweet curves of her breasts and the warm, sleek line of
her thighs, a deep groan shook his body as he urgently
parted her legs. Lorna cried out with ecstasy at the hard
thrusting strength of his manhood which aroused such
a mindless, aching excitement within her, drowning in a
vast storm of passion as he brought them both to the
exquisite satisfaction of mutual fulfilment.

Lorna surfaced at the approach of dawn. The grey
morning light lit the room with a dim glow and she felt
the comforting weight of Alex's arm across her waist.
She felt totally relaxed and lethargic, her slim body
moving sensually as her mind filled with memories of
their lovemaking last night, and her own abandoned
response to Alex's experienced mastery of her emotions.
He must have felt her movement of remembered
pleasure as his arm tightened to draw her towards his
hard body, sleepily grunting with satisfaction at the feel
of her warm, pliant flesh so close to his.

When she opened her eyes again, Lorna found she was
alone. Turning her head, she saw the shafts of morning
sunlight streaming in through the window, the timepiece

beside Alex's bed telling her that it was almost eleven
o'clock. How could she possibly be still in bed at this
hour? Very easily—after last night! she told herself,
stretching her satiated, languorous body, her face
flushing as she recalled details of last night's passionate
encounter.

Deciding that she couldn't stay in bed all day, she rose
and went to have a shower. It was only when she was drying
herself later, and looking around for something to wear,
that she began to think about the realities of her situation.
Alex's lovemaking had been exquisite, but had he really
said he loved and wanted to marry her? Or had that been
the result of her heated imagination implanting what she
wanted to believe into her brain? And—and that was only
one of her difficulties. What about everyone back at
Oakeley Park? Did they know where she was, and with
whom? The crowd of questions filled her brain as she sank
down on the edge of the bed, prey once again to all the
uncertainties about herself and Alex which had
tormented her for so long.

Maybe she had made a monumental fool of herself
after all? She had been so emotionally exhausted by the
time they had arrived here last night, that she hadn't been
capable of resisting the driving force of her love for Alex,
completely discarding all the sense she had been trying to
instil into herself this last month. After their pleasure and
rapturous happiness last night she did not doubt that he
cared deeply for her. But—but for how long? What would
happen when another girl such as Luci appeared on the
scene, flaunting herself at Alex and inciting him into
wanting to possess her body? Lorna almost moaned
aloud at the thought, before forcing herself to get up and
take some fresh clothes from her suitcase.

Slipping into a simple green, woollen, cowl-necked
dress, which exactly matched the colour of her eyes, she
quickly pinned her hair into a loose coil at the nape of
her neck and completed her make-up in record time.

She must find Alex. Then, maybe, she would find out the answers to her questions.

Going downstairs, she wandered through the deserted house, disturbed at finding it empty, and beginning to feel increasingly awkward and unsure. What if Alex had decided to drive back to Oxfordshire? But surely he wouldn't have done so without leaving a note . . .? She tried to still the anxious questions tumbling through her mind, the rising panic as she realised that the house was completely empty. *Where was Alex?*

The fresh morning sunshine tempted her unhappy figure out into the small grass patio, and it was only then that she saw a small low building across the garden, its door open wide to the sun. Peering cautiously in, she heard a voice in the distance and moving towards it, realised that she was in Alex's studio. Tripods and lighting equipment were scattered about, while the walls were hung with copies of his most famous portraits. Although she would have liked to linger over them, she was far too impatient to find the studio's owner. Pushing open a door that was already ajar, she saw Alex's tall figure dressed in an old pair of jeans and a blue short-sleeved shirt. He was standing with his back to her, looking out of a window and talking to someone on the phone.

'Yes, darling, there is absolutely no problem. I've just got a small matter to clear up here, first of all, and then I'll be with you.' He laughed, and listened to what the person was saying on the other end of the line. Lorna couldn't hear the words, but she could make out a woman's voice, and cold fingers of fear clutched her heart as she heard the rest of the conversation. 'Yes, darling, I promise that I won't be long. No, I can't wait to see you again, either. 'Bye love.'

Alex put down the receiver, and turned to see Lorna standing in the doorway, gazing at him shocked and white-faced as if she had seen a ghost. 'Who—who were you talking to . . .?' she asked in an agonised whisper.

Alex stood looking at her for a long time, all expression fading from his face, his eyes becoming hard and unreadable as the silence lengthened between them. 'Well now—that's an interesting question, isn't it? I wonder who you think it was, Lorna?' he drawled slowly.

'How—how should I know?' she protested huskily.

'But you immediately suspected the worst—didn't you,' he probed. 'Despite all that passed between us last night, it was clear from your face that you believed I was making an assignation with another woman, hmm?'

'No! No—I . . .' Lorna's voice trailed away as she tried to rationalise and understand her overwhelming feeling of panic at this phone call. Was he right? Was that what she'd thought?

'I think,' he said slowly, 'yes, I really think that I'm going to let *you* decide the matter.' He gave her a wry, bitter smile. 'Perhaps you can tell me who you think was on the phone?'

She stared at him in mounting panic. He wasn't just asking her an idle question. He was forcing her to make a fundamental and final choice about their relationship—both now and in the future.

'Oh, yes, Lorna, you're quite right!' His words confirmed her worst fears. 'Here and now, it's come to the crunch between us, hasn't it? Do you really think that I'm the sort of man who is capable of making an assignation with another girl, only hours after making love to you? Or was I talking to an old friend—or the butcher—or my mother—or maybe an old flame . . .? The list is endless, isn't it?' he sighed heavily.

'It's no good, you see. My darling love, I can't face the dreadful agony and the rows we would have, with you always expecting the worst and accepting as gospel truth any stupid rubbish printed in the newspapers. I'd never dare to even talk to another woman, would I? Mindless, unnecessary jealousy will rust and corrode any reationship in the end. Neither of us would want that, would we?'

Lorna stood staring at him, the blood frozen in her veins, as Alex walked over and took her hands in his, drawing her trembling figure into the room. 'Look around you, darling,' he murmured, her eyes widening as she saw that the walls of his office were covered with photographs of her face—large, blown-up copies of the shots he had taken in his studio.

'My adorable Lorna,' he said, 'I told you last night that I loved you. I said that I wanted to marry you . . . and live with you for the rest of my days. My sweet idiot! Surely you must know that I experienced total ecstasy and joy in your arms last night . . .? How can you possibly doubt my deep love and devotion . . .?' He paused, looking down into her dazed, slanting green eyes. *So, who do you think I was talking to, Lorna?*

Gazing up into his eyes, her mind was full of scattered, flickering images. Alex's determined pursuit despite her rebuffs, both here in England and New York; the kindness not only for his cousins and his mother, but even extending to his dreadful aunt; his patience with her doubts and uncertainties; the tender concern when she had got wet in the rain and—above all—the overwhelming love she had for the man whose hands trembled slightly as he stared down at her with harsh, brooding intensity.

'Well . . .?' Alex demanded impatiently.

Lorna took a deep breath, realising the truth behind Lady Caroline's words—that nothing was ever safe or sure in life. Nothing, but the knowledge of their deep love for each other. Suddenly, all the painful knots loosened inside her mind, leaving her free of all doubts and uncertainties . . . and totally sure of her decision. 'Darling, Alex—what a question!' she murmured. 'You were talking to the *butcher*—of course! Who else would you be calling "darling" at this time of the day?'

'You witch!' Alex groaned as Lorna collapsed against him, helpless with laughter. 'You know what you are, don't you?' he shook her roughly in the release of his pent-up tension.

'Oh, yes,' she said, laughing up into his eyes. 'I'm the woman who hasn't said that she's going to marry you yet—that's who I am!'

'Oh, my darling,' he breathed. 'I love you so much, I—I felt like shooting myself after that row we had in your bedroom. I—well, I was devastated. I'd tried everything I could think of, and you still didn't trust me an inch. I'd thrown up my work and hurried over from New York for one last, desperate attempt at wooing you—but everything went wrong! I think I'd have given up if it hadn't been for my mother. God! She came storming into my room last night like an avenging fury! Telling me that I had behaved like a complete idiot, and that thanks to my inept handling of the situation between you and I, she was in danger of losing a perfectly marvellous daughter-in-law! I'd never seen her so cross . . .' he shook his head in rueful amusement. 'I must confess that it was her idea that I drive you up to London, with the injunction not to make such a damn stupid mess of what was obviously my last chance. She was absolutely livid with me, and what with you flinching whenever I looked at you—it was enough to put me off women for life . . .!'

'You? Off women . . .? Hah!' Lorna snorted, her shoulders shaking with laughter.

'My love,' he said softly. 'I—well, I am thirty-six and I have been around for a while. You seem to have the most extraordinary view of my past—er—love life! But I would be a little odd, to say the least, if I hadn't been involved with some women in my time, hmm? However, I give you my solemn word that I have never heedlessly seduced anyone, neither have I ever taken a young girl's virginity—both of which I would regard as a crime. Please believe me?'

'Yes, darling, of course I do,' she replied simply.

'Right—that's enough of that,' he said with relief in his voice. 'Now, are you going to marry me? You'd better say yes, or I shall look a complete fool! As I'm sure you've guessed,' he grinned, 'that was my dear mama on the telephone. I was just telling her that she could go ahead and tell everyone the good news—she's particularly looking forward to informing Aunt Sophie! I also gave instructions to the effect that, since Jacques brought that awful girl Luci down, he could damn well get rid of her, *immediately* . . .!'

'Hang on—I've just remembered my work.' Lorna looked up at him in dismay. 'What on earth am I going to do about that?'

'Not much, since from now on I'm going to be the only photographer you'll ever see! I know what goes on in some of those studios!' he said darkly. 'What's more, that business about modelling for shop mannequins is *absolutely* out! I'm damn well not going to have my wife appearing in every shop window . . .! And while I'm laying down the law, I must say that although I was immensely encouraged by your jealousy of Luci . . .' he laughed as she blushed and hung her head, 'if you ever see that revolting man, Jay Holden, ever again—I won't be responsible for my actions! However, we'll have fun with Mercy's Get Fit project together, won't we? But, my dearest Lorna, you'll have to face the fact that it's strictly kisses, kids and kitchen for you in the future. Now, you gorgeous girl, don't you think that it's time you took pity on me?' he demanded huskily. 'Please say that you'll marry me . . .?'

'Oh, yes!' Lorna breathed, putting her arms around his neck. 'I'm not bad in a kitchen, and I'm longing to have your children, but in the meantime, *loverboy*—do you think we could possibly start on the kissing straight away . . .?'

You're invited to accept 4 books and a surprise gift Free!

Acceptance Card

Mail to: Harlequin Reader Service®

In the U.S.
2504 West Southern Ave.
Tempe, AZ 85282

In Canada
P.O. Box 2800, Postal Station A
5170 Yonge Street
Willowdale, Ontario M2N 6J3

YES! Please send me 4 free Harlequin Presents® novels and my free surprise gift. Then send me 8 brand new novels every month as they come off the presses. Bill me at the low price of $1.75 each ($1.95 in Canada)—an 11% saving off the retail price. There are no shipping, handling or other hidden costs. There is no minimum number of books I must purchase. I can always return a shipment and cancel at any time. Even if I never buy another book from Harlequin, the 4 free novels and the surprise gift are mine to keep forever.   108 BPP-BPGE

_____
Name   (PLEASE PRINT)

_____
Address   Apt. No.

_____
City   State/Prov.   Zip/Postal Code

This offer is limited to one order per household and not valid to present subscribers. Price is subject to change.   ACP-SUB-1

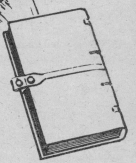